"Rather than put Nazarine through countless pointless battles of succession, I must marry immediately and do my best to procreate before my brother does."

Felipe looked straight at her. Into her. She had the sensation that her heart was falling down a flight of stairs and he was watching it happen.

"I don't understand," she said carefully.

"Of course you do. You know exactly where I'm headed because you're very smart, Claudine. It's one of the things that attracts me to you."

"No. It— I— No." Her ears were ringing. "You can't be serious, Felipe. No."

"I am very serious, Claudine. I want you to marry me."

Canadian **Dani Collins** knew in high school that she wanted to write romance for a living. Twenty-five years later, after marrying her high school sweetheart, having two kids with him, working at several generic office jobs and submitting countless manuscripts, she got The Call. Her first Harlequin novel won the Reviewers' Choice Award for Best First in Series from *RT Book Reviews*. She now works in her own office, writing romance.

Books by Dani Collins

Harlequin Presents

One Snowbound New Year's Night
Innocent in Her Enemy's Bed

Four Weddings and a Baby

Cinderella's Secret Baby
Wedding Night with the Wrong Billionaire
A Convenient Ring to Claim Her
A Baby to Make Her His Bride

Jet-Set Billionaires

Cinderella for the Miami Playboy

The Secret Sisters

Married for One Reason Only
Manhattan's Most Scandalous Reunion

Visit the Author Profile page
at Harlequin.com for more titles.

Dani Collins

AWAKENED ON HER ROYAL WEDDING NIGHT

HARLEQUIN
PRESENTS

HARLEQUIN®
PRESENTS™

ISBN-13: 978-1-335-59179-1

Awakened on Her Royal Wedding Night

Copyright © 2023 by Dani Collins

Harlequin Enterprises ULC
22 Adelaide St. West, 41st Floor
Toronto, Ontario M5H 4E3, Canada
www.Harlequin.com

Printed in U.S.A.

AWAKENED ON HER
ROYAL WEDDING NIGHT

CHAPTER ONE

"You'll die out there!" the Prince shouted from his speedboat. "I'm not coming after you!"

Good, Claudine Bergqvist thought, even though the sea was cold enough that her muscles were already cramping. The water was dark and pulled at the maxi-dress she wore. The jersey silk tangled against her legs as she tried to frog-kick. Waves dipped and rolled, making it hard to catch her breath without taking in a mouthful of water.

She was swimming a breaststroke so she could keep her vision fixated on the island ahead of her, but even though she was a strong swimmer, that black rise of land with only a few twinkling lights upon it was still terrifyingly far away. Barbed hooks of panic were trying to take hold in her while her imagination ran away with her. What else lurked in these waters besides her and that horrible man who had lured her onto his boat?

She heard the engine start up and stopped to

tread water, swiveling to see if he was coming after her.

No. The running lights turned away from her. The aerodynamic speedboat shot away in a burst of its engine, spewing froth behind it.

She couldn't see the yacht that had birthed it, or the super yacht where she had started her evening. This whole night had been a nesting doll of ever more perilous situations, not that she had seen it at the time.

"Come to a big party on a big boat. Why don't some of you come to a smaller party on my smaller yacht? Actually, let's take my runabout for a spin, just you and me."

Now it was just him, the Prince, heading back to Stella Vista, the biggest island in the chain that made up the Kingdom of Nazarine. And her, Claudine. Alone in the sea.

Her heart thumped erratically. Her abdomen tightened with so much anxiety her lungs could barely draw a breath. The wake from the departing speedboat rippled toward her, picking her up and dropping her into the trough so she lost sight of the boat.

When she spun in the water, the small island she'd seen a moment ago was gone.

She turned and turned.

Do not panic.

There it was. She kept her gaze pinned to it

while she fought the clinging material of her dress. She pulled her arms from its straps before she pushed the sheath off her waist and hips, freeing herself of the encumbrance.

I can do this.

She had done many things that were difficult, including becoming the Swedish contestant in the Miss Pangea pageant despite living in America for the last fifteen years.

She had also once won a bronze medal for her breaststroke. She'd been eleven and it had been a medley relay. Her portion had only been one hundred meters, but her team had made it to the podium.

Mom needs me alive, she reminded herself as she resumed her kick, stroke, breathe.

The thought of her mother only made her more anxious, though. Ann-Marie Bergqvist hadn't wanted Claudine to do this pageant. Not any pageant. They were archaic and sexist, she'd insisted.

They were, Claudine agreed, but she'd stumbled into the first one on a lark with friends, then kept winning. At first, she had competed for a scholarship and some trendy clothes. Then luggage and a vacation in the Caribbean. She had been flattered by the modest fame and the interviews with TV personalities, but when her mother's well-managed multiple sclerosis suddenly took a sharp turn into more serious symptoms, Claudine had sold the car she'd won along with the appliances.

The cash had bought her mother some time off work and a number of specialist appointments, but her disease was not one that could be cured, only managed. Each time Claudine leveled up and won a bigger pageant, she was able to afford better care for her mother.

The global Miss Pangea pageant was one of the most lucrative. It had brought her to Nazarine, near the ankle of Italy's boot, and if she was chosen to appear in their notoriously sexy swimsuit calendar, she would receive a very generous compensation. If she made the cover, she would earn even more. In fact, she was the favorite to win the whole contest.

If she made it to shore.

Was that why the Prince had targeted her? Because she was odds on to win?

She tried not to think of it. She was already tired. The exertion of swimming was not the problem. The force of the sea was taking a toll. This was no placid pool where she could skim along. She was being shoved from all angles, catching waves up the nose and swallowing salt water.

What if she didn't survive? What if she didn't make the photo shoot tomorrow? What if she didn't win any prize money and her mother had to let her disease run its course?

What if she drowned and never saw her mother again?

Don't think of it.

Kick, stroke, breathe. Kick, stroke, breathe.

"Intruder, Your Highness." Prince Felipe's guard brought him a tablet as Felipe was sitting down to a late dinner.

Francois.

His mind always leaped to his twin when something unpredictable and less than desirable happened. Cold hatred threatened to engulf him, but Felipe habitually banked those grim, unhelpful emotions. He focused on exactly what was happening in the moment.

"How many?" He took the tablet.

"Just the one, sir." The guard tapped to show the security footage in both night vision and infrared. A swimmer was approaching the western side of the island.

Situated furthest from the rest of the islands in the Nazarine archipelago, Sentinella had been named hundreds of years ago for the protective armies that had been stationed here. Its lofty cliffs allowed unimpeded surveillance of the surrounding waters and its lack of low, sandy beaches made it difficult to infiltrate.

In fact, any craft attempting to enter that particular lagoon took a beating through a toilet bowl of currents that punched every which way. Once inside, the shallow cove was littered with sharp rocks that lurked below the surface. They shipwrecked vessels and were guaranteed to shred a knee if you didn't know where they were. There was no reward once you reached the beach at the base of the cliffs. It was mostly rocks and coarse sand.

Like its occupant, Sentinella was formidable and inhospitable to strangers.

Felipe tried to expand the image, but it was too grainy to provide many clues as to the swimmer's identity.

"How did they get here? Is there a vessel nearby?"

"The *Queen's Favorite* held a sunset dinner for the pageant contestants this evening. Tenders were buzzing around it, bringing people back and forth from Stella Vista and taking side trips to the smaller islands. That's normal for these things. There was a seven-meter speedboat stalled about a mile out an hour ago. That's the closest any came to us."

The guard's lips were tight. He knew the hostility that existed between the Princes and hated to even mention Francois.

Felipe wasn't ambushed by the news that his brother was nearby. Francois spent most of his life chasing skirt and parties around the globe, but he always came home at this time of year, bringing his sordid little beauty contest to their island kingdom.

He didn't usually send trespassers boldly up to Felipe's front door, though. Not when he had his image and his own personal interests to protect. What was he up to this time?

"Let's greet our visitor." Felipe rose without having tasted the braised duck before him.

"Sir, he might be armed."

He? Felipe looked again at the screen. The swimmer had found a rock to clasp. As their arm came out of the water, the strap of a bikini top was revealed.

"Unless she intends to spit a cyanide capsule at me, I don't think she's carrying a weapon." He strode out the door to the inner grounds of the castle fortress, then across to the gate in the wall.

Two guards followed him, radioing low communications to the rest of the team. Another two fell into place next to Felipe as he stepped beyond the wall of the castle and made for the second gate, the one that blocked access to the stairs down the cliff face.

The narrow steps had been chipped from the stone wall by long-ago soldiers. A weathered rope was mounted through eyelets pounded into the rock, providing a tenuous handhold if a foot happened to slip.

Felipe hadn't been down these steps in years, never at night, but he waved away the guard who tried to illuminate the path with a handheld spotlight. He wanted to approach more stealthily.

The quarter moon made it a treacherous descent. When they came to the bottom of the stairs, cypress trees briefly blocked his view of the water. He could hear the waves fighting one another outside the lagoon, but also heard a feminine cough and some ragged breathing near the shore.

He brushed past the guard who held out an arm, trying to hold Felipe back from advancing the short distance to the water's edge.

In the pale moonlight, a woman—a mermaid? a siren?—was crawling from the glittering, black water. She paused, rearing up so she knelt in the shallows. Water lapped around the tops of her thighs. Her hair was pewter in the moonlight and stuck in vine-like curls against her shoulders and chest. Silver droplets fell off her chin and sat like diamonds against the swells of her breasts before slithering down her abdomen. Her chest heaved and every breath held a sob of effort.

That wasn't a bikini. It was a bra and underwear, a lacy set in an indeterminate color that sat as a charcoal streak against skin that might have been tanned golden or naturally tawny, but in the cool light of the moon, turned her into a timeless black-and-white photo of a castaway survivor. Of Venus, rising from the deep.

She was the most fiercely beautiful thing Felipe had ever seen. She made his guts twist in a mix of awe and lust, the desire to possess and an instant certainty that she could not be captured or contained.

In a surge of uncharacteristic jealousy, he wanted to physically knock his guards' gazes away from her. She was *his*.

With a fresh moan of effort, she crawled further out of the water and collapsed onto her side, chest heaving, legs still in the lapping surf.

As Felipe strode toward her, he dragged his gaze from her long thighs and trembling abdomen, past the quiver of her breasts to the way her eyes popped open beneath the anguished knot of her brows.

"What are you doing here?" he demanded in the Nazarinian dialect of Italian, crouching beside her.

The noise she made was one of pure suffering. Her arm moved in a sudden arc. A fistful of gravel peppered his face.

How was he *here*?

It didn't make sense, but Claudine didn't think, only reacted, trying to get away from the devil himself. She closed her hand on whatever bits of shells and rocks were on this godforsaken excuse for a beach and threw it at him.

While he swore roundly, she tried to roll away from him and get her arms and legs under her, but her muscles were utterly exhausted. She was shaking and weak, disoriented.

In the same moment, there were shouts and a scuffle of noise. A harsh male voice barked something in Italian. A heavy, rough weight pressed onto the back of her shoulder, squashing her onto her own feeble arms.

She should have let the sea take her because she was going to die tonight regardless of her fight to live. She let her face droop onto the pebbled beach beneath her.

I'm sorry, Mom. You were right. I'm so sorry.

There was a potent moment of silence, one that made her realize she had spoken aloud.

A burst of authoritative Italian came out of the Prince. There was the sound of a dull slap that transmitted a vibration into her shoulder before the punishing weight lifted off her back. It had been a foot, she realized, one with a roughly treaded sole. That's all she could see when she lifted her head. Boots and more boots.

"Don't attack me again," the Prince warned in his accented English. "My guards don't like it."

If only *she* had guards, she thought with brief

hysteria. Instead, she had been one woman defending herself against *his* attack.

She tried to push herself into sitting up and facing him, but her arms were overcooked pasta, completely ineffectual. Every part of her hurt. She didn't even have the strength to cry.

"How did you get here?" he asked.

That seemed too obvious to bother answering. She searched for a path of escape, but only saw boots, boots, rocks and more boots. Then feet in what had to be bespoke Italian shoes. Not deck shoes like the Prince had been wearing earlier. Laced leather shoes with fancy detailing.

She could still hear the swish and churn of the water at the mouth of the lagoon. Soft waves were caressing her calves. Dare she try that route again? Swimming had been her only escape the first time, but she hadn't managed to escape him, had she?

With a sob of utter despair, she dropped her head onto her wrist.

"Why are you here?" he prodded.

Seriously?

"I was aiming for Sicily. Is this not it?" she asked in a rasp.

There was a smirk from one of the hovering guards. The aggressive one who'd stood on her earlier nudged her hip with the toe of his boot.

"Don't be smart. You're under arrest. Answer the Prince's questions."

The Prince, whom she heartily consigned to the hottest corner of hell, said something in quiet, lethal Italian that had all of his guards shuffling back a few steps.

"Now," the Prince continued in English, "if you want to lie here waiting for all your cuts to grow septic, we can do that. Or you can come up to the castle for medical attention and give me a full explanation for your presence here. Can you stand?"

He started to take hold of her arm, but a fresh surge of pure adrenaline, the kind with its roots in an atavistic desire to survive, knocked his hand away. She scrabbled for a fresh handful of sand to throw at him.

"No." His knee went into the bed of pebbles in front of her eyes while his firm hand pinned her wrist to the ground. The other immobilized her bent arm against her chest, pressing her onto her back. "We've talked about that."

She was dimly aware of a noise that she had only heard in movies. It was the sound of guns being cocked and readied for firing. She had never been so petrified in her life. Her heart ought to have exploded.

She refused to look at him, though. She stared at the crease that went down the front of his trousers, from his knee to his shoe. Out of her well of pure hatred, she said, "Don't. Touch. Me."

"Open your hand," he commanded.

"Go to hell."

"We're staying here, then?"

She hated him. Really truly hated him.

But when his hold on her wrist didn't relent, she reluctantly allowed her fingers to splay. Her only weapon sifted out of her grasp.

His hold on her lifted away. "Can you stand on your own?"

She could not, but she refused to admit it. "I'm not going anywhere with you ever again," she choked. "I'd rather drown."

There was such a profound silence at that statement she opened her eyes and glanced around, half expecting the guards to have somehow evaporated.

"You were on the *Queen's Favorite*?" the Prince demanded.

"You know I was." She was really at the end of her rope. The salt on her cuts was killing her and her stomach was no longer tolerating all the seawater she'd swallowed.

"You swam the whole way from there? Impossible."

"Well, I didn't have a life ring or anything else to help me, did I? What sort of vile person leaves someone alone in the open water? At *night*?" The force of her emotive outburst put pressure on her stomach. Reaction to all that had happened—and all that she now faced—was starting to hit her with shattering force. She was definitely going to vomit.

"Porta la luce." He snapped his fingers.

One of his guards came forward to blind her with the light of a hideously strong torch. She flinched and tried to duck away from it, but the Prince took hold of her arm again and forced her to stay on her back.

It hurt like hell, but he ruthlessly kept her there and said, "Look." He pointed at the white line on his cheek. "Did I have this scar when you saw me last?"

"No."

Oh no...oh no. She had thought there was nothing worse than being trapped and preyed upon by the Prince of Nazarine.

There was one thing worse, though. One man worse. The *other* Prince.

"I am Felipe. Crown Prince of Nazarine. You will come up to the castle and tell me everything that happened tonight." He rose and offered his hand. "Can you walk? Or shall I carry you?"

She couldn't answer. It took all her strength to roll away so she wasn't violently sick all over his pretty shoes.

CHAPTER TWO

FELIPE SIGNALED HIS men to turn their backs and gently lifted her wet hair until it was behind her shoulders, then he supported her while she returned half the lagoon to its rightful owner.

When she'd finished retching, he drew her to sit braced between the V of his bent legs.

"Lean on me," he insisted while he removed his shirt.

She was trembling, likely in shock. Her long cold marathon of a swim was something even he, with his very athletic habits, would hesitate to attempt. It would also be taking a mental toll.

She was like a cloth doll, boneless as he threaded her arms into his sleeves. He brushed at sand on her shoulder which caused her to flinch, making him realize the skin beneath was scraped raw. Her shins wore similar injuries and there was a dark stain coming through on the elbow of his shirt.

He carefully closed two buttons between her

breasts, concentrating on that task rather than letting himself fully take in what she had put herself through to get away from Francois. That reckoning would come later, after he'd had a full account from her.

He gathered her in his arms and stood. She was long and lean and essentially a dead weight because she was so spent. Barely conscious, he suspected.

His head guard glanced warily over his shoulder, having been warned that one more step out of line—like *stepping on her again*—would cost him his job. His life, if they had lived a short century or two ago.

"A sling is on its way, sir," the guard said, taking a tentative step toward Felipe, arms outstretched.

Felipe shook his head, rejecting the man's attempt to help. He carried her to the bottom of the steps where he met the men who had brought the rescue sling. He gently placed her on it, draped a foil blanket across her and secured her with the straps.

"What is your name?" he asked as he worked. "Is there someone we should call?"

"I want to go home," she said with a pang of longing in her voice.

"I'm sure you do." Pity rose in him. He knew what it was like to be a target of Francois. His brother was cruel enough to enjoy terrorizing someone and dangerous enough to kill them in the process.

Felipe used one bent knuckle to caress her cheek soothingly. "Let's attend to your injuries first. Then we'll talk about what happens next."

She turned her head away from him and closed her eyes in rejection.

That shouldn't have bothered him, but it did. It was proof that Francois continued to leak poisonous lies about him and that people continued to believe them. Usually he didn't care, but he found himself bothered that *she* believed them.

Così è la vita. Such is life.

He took up one of the handholds of the sling himself, helping to carry her up the cliffs, then inside the castle walls to the infirmary.

Claudine woke in a dimly lit room. She was in a hospital bed with an IV tube stuck into the back of her hand, but the room looked like a five-star hotel. A Tiffany-style lamp stood on a Renaissance-style night table. Judging by the closed drapes, there was an adjoining terrace of some kind. Two wingback chairs faced a big-screen television above the mantel of a fireplace.

Was she back on Stella Vista? Thank God!

She tried to sit up and couldn't help the guttural noise that came out of her. Every muscle protested as though thoroughly bruised. She grabbed at the bed rail, trying to pull herself up, only to watch a specter-like shadow rise from a wingback and come toward her.

Her heart tripped and her throat went dry, making it impossible to swallow.

"Good morning," Felipe said. He was even more imposing in the weak daylight, wearing a crisp white shirt and gray trousers. His dark hair was short and precise. His jaw was shiny with a fresh shave.

That scar on his cheek was both reassuring and terrifying. He wasn't Francois, but what kind of man was he? What did he intend to do with her?

She sank back onto her pillow.

"My medical staff cleaned your injuries and topped up your fluids." Felipe nodded at the IV bag, then pressed the back of his fingers to her forehead and cheek.

A teetering sensation arrived in her midsection. *Don't trust him*, her logical mind cautioned. A more instinctual side of her yearned for someone to look after her.

"No fever. That's good." He reached across her to press a button, filling her senses with the spicy fragrance of aftershave. "Our guest is awake," he said, then released the button and straightened. "Are you hungry?"

"What time is it?" Her voice came out raspy and weak.

He turned his head to look at where a clock hung on the wall. "Six twenty."

Time enough to make the photo shoot? She was supposed to be there by eight.

"Dr. Esposito." The Prince greeted the man who came into the room. "Did you sleep in your clothes?"

"In case I was needed, yes." The doctor looked to be in his seventies. He stifled a yawn as he buttoned his white coat over his creased clothing. "Good morning, Claudine. How are you feeling? Are you in pain?"

"How do you know my name?" She darted her gaze back to Felipe.

"My security team are all highly trained operatives who employ the latest technologies in facial recognition," Felipe told her impassively. "None of which was necessary. I looked up this year's Miss Pangea contestants and there you were, second from the left."

"Your pulse is elevated," the doctor said, holding her wrist while watching the clock. "The Prince has been known to have that effect on a woman. Should I ask him to step out of the room?"

Was that supposed to be a joke? Felipe seemed to think so. His eyelids floated down over his dark brown eyes, heavy with amusement.

She sealed her lips. If she said yes, it would confirm she was reacting to him. If she said no, it would seem as though she wanted him to stay.

It's *fear*, she wanted to spit at him. Contemptuously.

As if he read her mind and was deeply unimpressed, the smug curl at the corner of his mouth deepened.

"I have to use the bathroom," she told the doctor. "Can you take this out of my hand?"

He made a noise of agreement and slid open a panel above her where supplies were kept. He unplugged the IV tube, smoothly removed the cannula and pressed a ball of cotton over the puncture, taping it in place.

He would have lowered the bed rail then, but Felipe swiftly did it on the other side.

"I'll call the nurse to help," Dr. Esposito offered.

"I can manage," Felipe insisted.

"I think he was talking to me," Claudine said, annoyed that one light brush of the Prince's hand was all it took to swing her legs off the bed while his other arm effortlessly slid behind her back, bringing her to sit on the edge facing him.

The abrupt move made her head swim so she wound up bracing a hand against his chest and clinging to his sleeve, waiting for her equilibrium to catch up to the rest of her.

"He was not," Felipe assured her. His firm hand on her waist ensured she didn't topple forward off the bed. "The nurse is also a man, so there's no difference in who helps you except that Dr. Esposito suffered a back injury last year, so he should not."

There was every difference, she wanted to grouse. She didn't want to be near him anymore than his brother.

She slid off the bed and her knees almost gave out.

Felipe caught her.

Dear *Lord*, she hurt. How was it possible to be this wrecked and still be alive?

She clung to his arms, needing his support to stand. She felt a thousand years old as she shuffled to the bathroom, every footstep sending a lightning bolt through her stiff muscles.

His arm stayed firm across her back while his fingers dug into her waist. Heat radiated off his torso through his shirt and the hospital gown she'd been put into. She could have cried at that invasion, being stripped and touched by strangers.

One glance at his indifferent profile and she doubted he had stuck around to watch. His brother might have leered in that circumstance, but Felipe didn't seem to see her as a woman at all.

"Can you manage?" he asked briskly as he lowered her onto a velvet bench beside the toilet.

"Yes."

Even this bathroom, which was clearly still part of the medical wing, was beautifully appointed with gold fixtures, a claw-foot tub, and a huge shower stall tiled in dark blue. On the back wall of the shower tiles, a landscape of a coastal village sat inside a painted frame of golden grape vines.

"Don't even *think* of going through that window." He pointed to the panel of stained glass inserted into a modern casement that allowed it to swing outward. "You'll land on the guard stationed below."

She had absolutely been thinking of doing that. He probably knew it from the belligerent dismay that came into her face at his warning.

"Call if you need me." He left her alone.

She used the toilet since she'd come all this way, then washed her hands before she took inventory of her injuries. Four scrapes had bled enough to need covering, two on her shins, one on her shoulder and one on her forearm. The rest were scuffs that had been painted with something that had stained her skin yellow. There was even a small bruise on her cheekbone.

As she met the appalled disbelief in her reflection, all she could think was, *I can't do the photo shoot. I can't win.*

She had been in the top three in every portion

of the contest so far. She was the frontrunner who was expected to win.

Not anymore.

It's over.

Mom...

As long as Claudine could remember, her mother had had good spells and bad spells, but her symptoms had always receded. This time, they were more severe and weren't going away. Ann-Marie was in a lot of pain and having trouble walking. She seemed to be losing vision in one eye.

After two decades of coping with it, Ann-Marie had exhausted all the conventional treatments. She had gone into a secondary progressive phase, her doctor had told her. There were experimental treatments that were showing promise, like stem cell transplants, but they were expensive and held out no guarantees. However, without any sort of treatment, she would definitely suffer more pain, keep losing function, and her life span would be shortened.

Claudine's gamble on winning the prize money hadn't been a sure bet, but it had been a strong one. Even something like being chosen for the calendar would have given her enough money to hire her mother a specialized home care worker.

What would she do now?

With a sob of despair, Claudine sank back onto

the bench, hands covering her face only to discover there was still enough sand in her hair to rain onto her knees. Her feet were filthy, her pedicure a disaster.

She didn't think about whether it made sense to shower, only rose to start the water. She dropped the gown and stepped under the spray, reaching for the shampoo. She washed her hair, then rubbed the silky body wash all over her skin, trying to remove salt and dirt and this whole wretched experience.

Maybe the scrapes could be covered with makeup, she thought wildly. As the water soaked through the bandages, she peeled them away, finding long red streaks and skin scraped raw. It would scab even worse before it healed.

The soap stung like living hell, but she scrubbed anyway, trying to erase the scratches and scuffs with the fluffy white cloth only to stain the soft cotton with fresh blood.

Would the pageant even pay to fly her home? Francois would probably accuse her of walking away and disqualify her. He'd been furious when she had fought off his advances.

"Do you want to win or don't you?"

What should she do? Report him? Who would believe a prince had left her to die in the open sea?

She cringed, realizing that even if she could convince anyone she'd been on his speedboat at all, he would only turn it around and claim she had come aboard intent on seducing him to try and win the pageant. That she was a cheater. How had she been so *stupid*?

"Claudine." There was a firm knock.

She ignored him and kept scrubbing.

"Stop that." Felipe entered. "You're making it worse. Stop, Claudine. *Stop*."

He came right into the shower, ignoring the rain of the spray that soaked his clothes and landed on his gold watch. He snapped off the taps and stole the cloth from her hand, throwing it to the floor with a plop. Then he stepped away and reached for a towel. He shook it out and wrapped it around her trembling body, seeming to take no notice of the fact she was absolutely naked.

As he had done on the beach last night, he easily picked her up and carried her to the bench where he left her soggy and bedraggled and freshly bleeding.

"Give her new bandages," he said irritably as he walked out.

Claudine swallowed a lump in her throat. She was so irrationally bereft at his leaving she almost called out for him to come back.

A man she presumed was the nurse, since he wore scrubs and carried a tray of tape and bandages, used a second towel to dab her shoulders and arms and face and feet. He was efficient and kind, covering each of her injuries again, then offering a comb before saying, "I'll fetch a clean gown."

As she struggled to work the tangles from her hair while keeping her towel in place, he returned with a clean, dry hospital gown and an over-the-counter headache tablet.

"Would you like help dressing?" he asked after she had swallowed the pill.

"She can wear these." Felipe arrived wearing a dry shirt and fresh trousers. He carried a pair of silk pajama bottoms in dark green with a plain, navy blue T-shirt. "It's good you're almost as tall as I am. Leave us. I'll help her."

The nurse closed the door behind him.

Felipe lowered to one knee as he began to thread the pajama bottoms up her calves and thighs. "Stand," he ordered.

With a small catch of her breath, she did, bracing a hand on his shoulder to hold her balance.

He pushed the waistband the rest of the way up, reaching under the towel with that same dispassionate expression. He stood and lifted the drape of the towel to tie the drawstring, then gathered the T-shirt and slipped it over her wet head. He guided one arm and the other through the sleeves then waited for the shirt to fall down and cover her chest before he dragged the towel away.

"My slippers." He set them in front of her bare

feet. "Now we'll eat breakfast. I sense you're the type who is grumpy until you've had your coffee."

He wasn't wrong, but that wasn't why she shuffled so resentfully behind him, wincing with every step.

The warm shower and moving around, along with the tablet, were gradually easing some of the ache from her muscles, though.

He took her through an empty ward of a half dozen beds, then past a series of offices where faces glanced up before quickly getting back to whatever they were doing. There was a grand hall of some kind with sunlight streaming in through a dome of colored glass that drew her eyes upward. Stairs curved down from a gallery, but he ignored them. There was a mosaic in the floor beneath their feet, but she didn't get a chance to study it.

They arrived at a pair of open doors where guards stood sentry. He led her through a small foyer that let onto a parlor, then through a huge, formal dining room.

"Are we there yet?" she couldn't help asking.

"Soon." He didn't even glance back at her, but after passing through a small breakfast room, they finally emerged on a shaded terrace where a table was set for two.

Half a dozen staff hovered, eager to pull out chairs and pour coffee and lift silver lids to reveal poached eggs on beds of chopped peppers with herbs and olives atop toasted bruschetta slices.

Claudine was so hungry she barely made herself wait until Felipe waved an invitation for her to tuck in. Flavors of basil and butter and salt exploded on her tongue. Blood oranges appeared with grapes and fresh figs. She gobbled them down, then chased them with a sweet pastry and a second cup of coffee.

When he said, "Bring oatmeal," she realized he had stopped eating long before she had. How embarrassing.

"No. Thank you," she insisted. "I missed dinner." She had missed a lot of meals in the run-up to this pageant, but there was no need to make up for it in one sitting.

She self-consciously sat back only to wince at the various aches and bruises that connected against the quilted seat back.

She finally took a proper look at her surroundings. This terrace was on the ground floor overlooking a courtyard that contained a hedge maze of waist height. A fountain in the center whispered its steady pour of water.

The walls of the courtyard were three stories high and were covered in tangled, verdant vines. She couldn't see the sea or the collection of islands that made up Nazarine, only a thin layer of wispy clouds in an otherwise blue sky.

She looked at the castle behind her, spotting a number of terraces that probably afforded a view to the horizon.

"I don't wish us to be seen by any long-range lenses," Felipe said.

"Why?"

"Because knowledge is power. Right now, I know that you survived your swim, but my brother does not."

The lethal grit in his voice caused her heart to take a swerve.

He looked so much like his brother it was disconcerting. Aside from that stark white line in his swarthy cheek, he was Francois's match in height and build. They both had thick, dark brown hair and equally dark brown eyes beneath stern brows. Their long sloping cheeks were clean-shaven, their jawlines chiseled from granite, their mouths...

Here she saw the difference. The shape was the same with a peaked top lip and a thick, blunt line for a bottom one, but Francois's mouth was softer. He smiled often and quickly and wore a pout when he relaxed.

Felipe's mouth held the tension of discipline and command. He didn't need to charm to get what he wanted, she realized with a roll of uncertainty through her abdomen. He spoke and he received.

"I'd like to go back to Stella Vista," she said.

"You will. In time."

"My mother expects me to check in every day. She'll be worried if she doesn't hear from me soon." That was an exaggeration. "The organizers will be contacted."

"I'm counting on it." His mouth twisted with cruel satisfaction.

Her heart lurched. "Don't do that to her! She has enough to worry about."

Stress was the worst thing for her condition.

"We'll reassure her of your safety through private channels. Is there someone she trusts implicitly? One of these people who drives her to her medical appointments, perhaps?"

"How do you know that about her?" she asked with alarm.

"She thanked her team on social media. The post was set to public," he added when she recoiled. Warning flashed behind his eyes. "I was only trying to get to know my houseguest, not targeting her for anything."

A houseguest? Was that what she was? She hadn't exactly arrived voluntarily, and apparently wasn't allowed to leave. She searched the walls in the courtyard, spotting a door that led where? To a treacherous descent to the water and another life-threatening swim?

She curled her fingers into fists in her lap.

"Tell me about last night. How did you come to be in the water?"

She stubbornly clamped her mouth shut, not wishing to revisit it, especially not with servants and bodyguards standing around listening.

"Take your time. We can walk in the garden if you like. It's very relaxing."

She couldn't resist glancing at him then, wondering if he ever relaxed. He radiated readiness for action.

"I have never spent much time learning about the pageant." He casually held out his cup for someone to step forward and refill it. "I expect it's very competitive?"

"I was *not* trying to get an advantage!" she burst out, insulted. Her eyes immediately grew hot and she cast another annoyed glance at their audience.

"Go." He flicked his hand and they all melted away.

It helped that they were alone now, but would he even believe her? Defensive words bubbled up. She was desperate to plead her side of it before she had to face all the scrutiny and disbelief that would be heaped upon her if she reported it to the pageant, though.

"You started on the *Queen's Favorite*, I presume?" he prompted.

"For a dinner cruise, yes. The ship is huge. I was part of a group touring all the decks when the Prince caught up with us. He invited us onto a smaller yacht. It was inside the bigger one and already had champagne and photographers on board. I thought it was a surprise announcement that we'd made the calendar or something. Pageants do that, ambush us with big news so they can capture our reactions."

She had been so excited at that point, giving absolutely no thought to being in any sort of danger.

"It was still a really big boat," she continued. "They took us toward one of the other islands where we could see the sun setting. Once it was dark, I wandered around and the Prince found me. He said, 'Look, I have this little boat that won all these races. Let's pop aboard and zip around to surprise everyone.' It seemed harmless. *He* did. Then he steered it away from all the other boats and…"

She didn't want to continue.

He didn't move or speak, but she couldn't look at him to see what he was thinking. She was too embarrassed.

"I feel really stupid for trusting him, but he owns the pageant. He's a *prince*." According to the online accounts, the twins had been competitive when they were young, but Felipe had supposedly been the one with the violent streak. Francois was the forgotten spare who was sensitive and kind and only wished to make his country proud.

"You don't have to tell me what happened, Claudine," Felipe said gravely. "The fact you swam a mile to get away from him tells me all I need to know, but if he...hurt you, Dr. Esposito can do any necessary tests. They're helpful for prosecution."

Her stomach protested the heavy meal she'd put into it. She swallowed and shook her head.

"That's not necessary. He didn't—he was angry that I wouldn't go below with him and grabbed my arm." She rubbed where there was a shadow of a bruise on her wrist. "I managed to pull away and... I jumped overboard. It was a senseless thing to do. I realize that now." She covered her eyes. "I just reacted."

"I'm sorry you felt it was your only option. And I'm glad you survived it," he said in a tone that sounded sincere, but also severe enough to draw her nerve endings taut. "Do you think this is something he's been doing all along? Assaulting his contestants?"

She hadn't even thought of that, but of course this would have been Francois's modus operandi.

She flashed a look upward. Felipe's voice was concerned, but his narrow-eyed visage suggested there was something more calculating behind his interrogation.

"Why do you care? Because you see this as a weapon you can use against him?"

His expression didn't change, but the sweep of his gaze suggested he was reassessing her. He sipped his coffee, giving the impression he was considering how much to tell her.

"His ship is called the *Queen's Favorite* because he is. Our mother adores him." He sat back, lips twisting with weary disdain. "I've always thought the pageant very tawdry. Our mother supports his argument that the pageant showcases Nazarine's beauty, raising our profile and enticing tourists to visit long after the pageant is over. I can't deny there are economic benefits to it, but if this contest is a cover for his sex crimes, then it must be stopped."

She folded her arms across her middle, cupping her elbows.

"Judging by the way certain crew members behaved..." Her stomach turned as she recalled the way the purser's gaze had slid away from hers. "It's hard to describe, but they didn't seem surprised by his taking me out alone. I have a feeling that if I were to go back and say that he had plotted to assault me, the crew would say I seemed happy to go with him. In fact..." She cringed as she saw it in a new light. "The Prince made a point of saying *I* wanted to see how fast his speedboat could go." She covered her face again. "If I accused him of anything, he would say what you implied, that I was just trying to seduce him so I could win the pageant."

"Will anyone have noticed last night that you went missing?"

"Probably not. There were tenders going back and forth to shore all evening. Other people coming and going. Celebrities and entertainers. It was very chaotic. They probably won't notice I'm missing until this morning's photo shoot for the calendar."

Her stomach was churning over that. She had never broken a contract in her life, but here she was missing one of the key requirements of the contest.

It was killing her that she had lost so much so quickly! She should have done as her mother had asked and taken the job at the bank. It was entry level and hadn't paid much. Not enough to support her mother or pay for her treatment. Definitely not both, but she could at least have been *with* her mother.

She'd been so sure she had a shot at that stupid calendar, though! It was easy money. Just *smile*.

"*Please*, can I go home?"

CHAPTER THREE

FELIPE HAD BARELY SLEPT. His mind had been busy running through every scenario and course of action available to him, now that such an odd, and potentially explosive, opportunity had washed up on his doorstep.

He needed more facts, though. And, as much as he had trained himself to be suspicious, he was keenly aware that he had to treat Claudine carefully. Her injuries were not faked. She had been through a terrible ordeal.

She was reassuringly stroppy, despite it. Perhaps because if it. For her sake, he was profoundly relieved she had foiled part of Francois's predatory plan, but he could see what the experience had cost her. She was physically wrecked and emotionally shaken.

Her mental toughness, however, glowed like a simmering star deep within her. It mesmerized him, not that he allowed his attraction to show. It wasn't appropriate under the circumstances. Also, her fear and hatred of his brother didn't mean Felipe could trust her. Any pull he felt toward her had to be ignored while he delved for the information he needed.

"I will make arrangements for you to go home in due course, Claudine. Right now, I want to know how you feel about calling out my brother for what he did. I realize that could be difficult for you on many fronts. That's why I'm asking, not insisting."

"What use would it do?" Her hands came up, palms empty and helpless. "He'll vilify me! I *might* get some modeling work after this, if I keep my mouth shut, but not if I'm seen as the type who makes waves. You're probably right about previous winners. I would tell you to go back and ask them, but I don't know if they can say anything, either. They would have to admit that their win was essentially a consolation prize after he took advantage of them. No, I just want to go home and try to forget any of this happened."

Her eyes were glistening as she stared at the far wall of the courtyard. She bit her lips to stop them from quivering.

"Claudine. I believe you," he said quietly. Firmly.

She sucked in a small breath and snapped her head around to stare at him, seeming to disbelieve *him*.

"That surprises you?" He frowned.

"Men in your position don't see how the world really works."

"We'll argue my comprehension of the world another time, but I assure you I know how my brother works." He paused to consider his words. "Perhaps that's inaccurate. I knew Francois objectified women. Other pageants have evolved to be less sexist, but Miss Pangea is appalling. I didn't ever imagine it was also a cover for Francois to commit sexual assault. Men in our position," he used the phrase ironically, "generally receive enough offers for companionship that we don't have to stoop to taking it by extortion or force."

Her mouth worked unsteadily, as if she was trying to find words and couldn't.

"I take responsibility for not stopping the pageant sooner. My dislike of it was seen as pettiness, so I allowed him to keep his toy. I'll insist this one be our last." It would widen the rift between himself and his mother. Their father would see it as another skirmish between his sons, taking accusations of Francois's crimes with a grain of salt. Ultimately, the King would side with canceling the pageant for the sake of the royal reputation, though.

"Losing the pageant will punish Francois," he continued, "but if you want him held accountable for his actions against you, that will require your testimony."

A tiny sob sounded in her throat. She looked down to pick at her broken fingernail.

"You don't have to decide this moment. I believe he'll be dissuaded from targeting another contestant if he's already stewing in the discomfort of one who has gone missing."

His brother really did think he was untouchable if he was prepared to leave a woman for dead. That news was very sobering and it pinched at Felipe's conscience that he had allowed himself to believe there were lines Francois wouldn't cross. He didn't think of himself as naive, but in this case, he had been.

"I imagine people will be asking for you at this photo shoot. When will your mother make inquiries? I would like my brother to begin fielding awkward questions as soon as possible."

"I text her updates through my day. She sees them when she gets up, but because of the time zones and how busy I am during the day, I usually only talk to her in my evenings. She—" Claudine hesitated, eyeing him as though wondering how much to trust him. "She knows I can get tied up with other things. She won't really worry until it's been a few days."

Felipe touched his phone. One of his security guards poked his head onto the terrace.

"Sir?"

"Use our back channels to offer generous payments for paparazzi shots of Claudine at the swimsuit photoshoot."

"When was the shoot, sir?" He glanced between her and Felipe.

"It's happening now."

"But—" He looked at Claudine, frowning at the obvious fact she was here, not there.

"I want photographers to ask the organizers why she's not among the contestants," Felipe spelled out. "If they see an opportunity for a generous reward, they'll then start looking for her elsewhere, stirring pots of curiosity as to why no one can find her."

"Ah." The guard nodded and retreated.

Claudine sent him a considering look.

"It's a start." He shrugged. "Let's walk in the garden. I think you'll find it soothing."

"I think I'll find it excruciating, but okay."

He bit back a grin of amusement, pleased by that spark of cheekiness in her. Her color was better and, despite a few winces as she rose, she was moving more fluidly, which also reassured him that, physically at least, she would bounce back from all of this.

Four stone steps took them down to the hedges that were trimmed to waist height.

"Do you know the way?" she asked.

"It's a meditative labyrinth. There are no dead ends, only one path. I walk it most days when I'm here. It helps me think." Which was something he needed to do now—contemplate exactly what to do with her.

He mentally scoffed at himself. He knew what he *wanted* to do with her, but he forcibly turned his mind from musing on that.

No, it was the conflict of seeing the means to finally destroy his brother and wanting to seize it, while also seeing a vulnerable woman who needed his protection, that needed untangling.

Testifying had to be her decision. He couldn't push her too hard on that front or he was no better than Francois, but the stakes were too high to not make an effort to persuade her.

She moved slowly on the graveled path, one hand reaching out to lightly graze the top of the boxwood, as though wading into water and testing the surface temperature as she went.

"The pageant is actually a very sharp tool in Francois's arsenal," Felipe said, wanting her to have a broader picture of his reasons for pressing her. "He makes a disgusting amount of money exploiting things like your image in a bikini."

Claudine frowned and crossed her arms defensively.

"He uses the selection events and the various whistle-stops as opportunities to mingle with diplomats and dignitaries. It looks harmless to the outsider, but he starts whisper campaigns against me. That's why my reputation is as sunny as it is," he said facetiously. "But it's useful for me to be seen as the more dangerous twin, so I don't mind."

Claudine made the first turn and looked back at him, brows pulled together in wary confusion. Her hair had dried and was straight as straw as it fell around her shoulders, casting out glints of gold in single, flyaway strands.

She was genuinely, naturally beautiful. He wasn't so shallow as to embrace classic attributes as an ideal, but he couldn't ignore the fact that her features were symmetrical, her eyes wide and clear, her lashes long and thick, accentuating her femininity. She had elegant bone structure and a mouth that was sensually plump and pursed at rest, as though ready for a kiss while the corners curled up in a secret smile. The rest of her was willowy and graceful, her curves filling out his clothing in a way that belonged on a runway despite the fact they were too big for her slender frame.

All of that appealed to him on a very base level, but beneath that was a quiet resilience that lit a fire in him. He didn't know why it made him want to grab her and hold her, while also revering her, but it did.

It was disturbing and he hid it all from her,

keeping an impassive expression on his face because she needed to trust he wouldn't harm her, otherwise she had no reason to help him.

"Francois labeled me the bully from an early age without thinking it through," he continued. "The result is that most people are more afraid of me than they are of him, adding to my influence and power. Which isn't to say I haven't done some terrible things to him. The story that I broke his nose when we were fifteen is true. In my defense, he tried to hit me with his car."

"That part isn't online." She slithered through two short zigzags and looked back at him again.

"My parents have kept his reputation as spotless as possible. He is the spare, after all. There is a small chance—although perhaps not that small given how much he hates me—that I might not survive to take the throne and he will ascend instead."

"I don't doubt that he tried to murder you," she choked. "I can't understand how your parents looked the other way, though."

"Our father encouraged our rivalry. He thought it made both of us stronger. Our mother coddled Francois, feeding into his sense of entitlement and resentment. When he acted out, attacking me, she defended him. Even when he did this—" He pointed at the scar on his face. "Lashing me with a sword before my mask was on. *I* was supposedly at fault for being unprepared."

"That's horrific."

It was. A millimeter deeper and he would have lost his eye.

They were passing each other on either side of a hedge, like people going opposite directions on a street. She stopped to study the scar. Her morbid curiosity caused a teetering sensation in his chest. He never let anyone touch it. It was remarkably sensitive, considering how long ago it had happened, but he had the sudden desire to feel her cool fingertips tracing every centimeter of it.

"I didn't ask for the responsibilities of the crown, but what is my choice? Allow a man with his lack of morals to rule our country? I can't. I'm not a particularly good man, but I know right from wrong. I'm in a constant struggle to hold my own against him without sinking to his level."

"If I did come forward, your parents would interfere to protect him. Isn't that what you're saying?" Dread pulled down the tilted corners of her mouth.

"You'll have my protection," he promised.

"What good will that do?"

They had come to the halfway point in the labyrinth. They stood outside the circle of hedge that surrounded the fountain, but would have to work their way through the second half to reach it.

"You understand those other contestants are my friends?" Her eyes dimmed with entreaty. "They all have hopes and dreams of their own. They're one step closer to those dreams because they participate in something like this. They wouldn't thank me for destroying the pageant when they're counting on whatever fame or attention they're able to get from it. And the past winners? They don't want to be put under microscopes. Helping you means harming others."

That almost sounded as though she had a conscience. He tested it.

"What if I pay you?"

"It's not about money!" Claudine turned in a huff and realized she was trapped. She couldn't go back, not without brushing past him, but the way forward was another pointless retreading of snaking paths.

She started through the next quadrant. He strolled behind her at his own pace, but she still felt pursued.

"There are easier ways to get money," she muttered over her shoulder. "I could have slept with your brother for the pageant prize if that's all I wanted!"

"That's what I keep coming back to. You've made a small career of these things. What is it you want from them? Fame? Adulation? A modeling career? Then pursue modeling."

"Not that it's any of your business, but I'm funding my mother's medical treatment."

"So it is about money."

"Not the way you're suggesting." She stopped to turn and confront him again, supremely annoyed and more than a little distressed by the gravity of her situation. "You probably saw online that my mother has multiple sclerosis. It has begun affecting her ability to work. She's managing some part-time hours from home, but she has to cover her insurance premiums herself. It's not very good insurance regardless. It only pays for the basics. Any kind of stress, especially financial, worsens her symptoms."

She paused to toe a loose rock in the otherwise trampled-flat gravel.

"If all she needed was someone to make meals and do her shopping, I'd move in with her and do that, but she's not responding to her usual medications. She needs a full reassessment and a whole new treatment plan. It'll cost the earth. Miss Pangea was only an eight-week commitment and I've had good luck with these things in the past, so I wanted to try. And yes—" she lifted her head "—I thought that if I could then move into modeling, that would be a better paying career than whatever entry-level job I'm barely qualified for, at least in the short term."

She hadn't been able to find her niche, career-wise. It was frustrating, but she kept trying things on, never quite sure what she hoped to find.

"Do you have other siblings? Does your mother have a partner?"

"No. I mean, she did. My moms were married and living in Sweden when they visited a fertility clinic to conceive me." People always had questions about this part of her life, so she answered before he asked. "The donor was an anonymous student who only gave two samples. Most men donate dozens of times and most prospective parents look for someone who has lots of samples in stock, in case it doesn't work right away. That way they don't have to go through the screening process again and again. My moms liked the rarity of this donor's sample so they each used one. One worked." She waved at herself.

"Theoretically, it's possible he had other children, though."

"Theoretically, yes. And it's a nice thought to imagine I have a half sibling out there and I might meet them through some divine intervention. Or my father."

"You've never tried to find him?"

"Not really." She wasn't bothered by how she had been conceived, but she did wonder some-

times if the piece of herself she didn't understand was the anonymous student. "The one time
I looked up the clinic, I learned it was closed and
the records destroyed. I've thought about doing
one of those DNA tests, but my mother… It's a
touchy subject. She did try to conceive another
child for our family, but it didn't work. After
Mamma died, I've always had the sense that if
I went looking for my donor, Mom would take it
as a criticism or a rejection. As though she wasn't
enough for me."

"She's not the one who carried you?" he asked.

"No. Mamma did. She died when I was eight.
Mom brought me to New York after, but we don't
have family there, either, so it's really up to me
to look after her."

She didn't know why she was bothering to tell
him her life story. She didn't care what he thought
of her. Did she?

"Those are all expenses I can cover," he said
mildly. "I'm a very rich man, Claudine."

He didn't have to sound so smug about it!

He was more than rich, though. He was enigmatic and intimidating, even though he only ambled along behind her, posing no immediate threat.

Which didn't mean she could trust him, she
reminded herself. He seemed to be treating her
well enough, but it was definitely for his own pur-
poses. She was essentially his hostage. As far as

she could tell, he wanted her to explode her own life—and that of every Miss Pangea contestant ever—so he could score a point or two with his brother.

Not that Francois didn't deserve to be knocked down. *He* was the one who was ruining her life. She knew that.

Felipe's talk of a whisper campaign had sounded a little paranoid, but now that she knew Francois was more—or more accurately *less*—than the charming, doting figurehead of the pageant he presented himself as, she had to wonder if she had believed what she had been told to believe about Prince Felipe. Maybe he wasn't as bad as advertised?

He was objectively good-looking, exactly like his brother, but Felipe had an edge. Not the scar. It was more than that. An aura. She was compelled to keep looking at him. Why? Was it the confidence bestowed by the power of his position? Something more intrinsic to him?

She didn't know what it was, but he fascinated her the way a shark or a deadly snake might hold her attention. She wanted to watch him move and listen to him tell her more about himself. She wanted his attention for no sane reason at all and she didn't want him to think badly of her. Why?

She paused, so close to the fountain she ought to be there by now, but she had to go through a final twist and turn, back and forth, to reach the opening to the inner garden.

"I don't know if I can believe anything you've told me," she said wearily as she came through the separation in the hedge. "Not when I'm just a means to an end for you."

Before her, rose bushes bloomed in a multitude of colors around a tiered fountain. Water poured off five concentric layers into larger pools below. The thin curtains of water were nearly silent, only creating a steady shush of sound while the gentle movement of the water wafted the perfume of the roses, heady and sweet, into the air.

Four curved benches were placed to view the fountain. She sat on the nearest one, sighing with relief. The walk had been longer and more taxing than she had expected.

"You would rather believe what Francois has told you?" Felipe idly picked a rose.

"I wouldn't believe him if he told me the earth was round," she muttered.

"Which is why I'm willing to align with you. My enemy's enemy is my friend." Felipe brought her the rose and offered it in the cup of his hand.

The stem was so short, there were no thorns. It was a beautiful blossom on the verge of opening. Each petal held bright yellow in its center that faded to peach and finally an intense pink at the furled edges.

It felt like an agreement of sorts to accept the rose, but it was too beautiful to refuse. She gathered it in her two hands, like scooping water, and found the brush of his palm against her knuckles disturbing. She brought the bloom to her nose where the soft, cool petals caressed her lips and the fragrance of nectarine and tea filled her nostrils.

"Do you really wish to slink back to Stella Vista, collect your things and fly home? And leave your friends to discover for themselves that Francois is a predator while you look after your mother on a shoestring?"

"I can't be paid to tell the truth." She lowered the rose into her lap. "That's wrong. If it came to light, it would completely undermine my claims. People would say you had bought my testimony." She stared at the fountain, feeling responsibility pouring onto her like the weight of that water, layer upon layer until she could hardly breathe. "I have to come forward. I know that. All of this..." She waved at the labyrinth and its singular path into its predetermined, unavoidable destination. "This was me coming to terms with the inevitable."

"It has that effect, doesn't it?" He tucked his hands into his pockets as he sent a contemplative look at the maze.

"I need time to gather my strength, though. I

can't do it right now." It was going to be awful. *So* awful. She would stay here forever if she could, inside the peace of a decision made, rather than travel out to execute it.

"Do you want me to help you? Carry you?"

He sounded solicitous, but his objective was to get the result he wanted. For some reason, that put a sting of tears on the edges of her eyelids.

"I can manage." She stood and turned toward the opening in the hedge, but swayed.

Instantly, he was in front of her, cradling her elbow in support.

She set her hand in the crook of his bent arm, tired and overwhelmed and needing to lean on his strength a moment.

His free hand skimmed down her hair, leaving a tingling path from her scalp over her ear, into the side of her neck and down her shoulder.

She jerked her head back, partly fearful, partly…something else. She was tall, almost six feet. He was taller. Tall enough to look down his nose at her.

"A butterfly was looking for a place to land."

She touched her hair.

"It's on the roses." He nodded.

She looked at the small yellow creature slowly fanning its wings as it sipped nectar.

"Are you afraid of me, Claudine?"

Yes. It was a visceral answer from the depths

of her being, but even as she thought it, her gaze clashed back into his and her heart turned over.

She *should* be afraid of him. More afraid than she really was.

Last night, with Francois, her inner alarms had been going off like mad from the time he had suggested the speedboat. She had ignored them, telling herself she was being silly. Francois was only trying to be nice.

Francois was not nice and neither was Felipe.

But Felipe wasn't trying to convince her he was nice. Nor was he being cruel. And even though logic was telling her to be cautious about trusting him, her inner alarms were rattled for other reasons. He had had ample opportunity to hurt her physically, but he hadn't.

No, the sting of danger in her nostrils was emotional wariness. He was slipping very easily past her normal defenses. She wanted to blame what she'd been through for making her feel weak and susceptible to him. It was probably a factor, but there was more at play. She was attracted to him.

Not just *Wow, he's hot*. It went deeper to *Who is he, really?*

He was making her long for things she had held at bay most of her life. Like most people, she carried an intrinsic desire to be loved, but she knew it was a double-edged sword. With love came the risk of loss. Loss of autonomy and self and the other person.

"You're safe with me. I hope you believe that." He set a crooked finger under her chin and tilted her face up to his.

He was barely touching her, only cradling her elbow and pressing that light touch under her jawline, but she felt as though he'd conducted an electric current through her, making all of her feel so tinglingly alive that her eyelashes fluttered under the force of it.

He narrowed his eyes and something like satisfaction spread across his watchful expression. His thumb brushed across her lower lip.

"I don't know what to believe," she admitted, trying to prevaricate. Trying to tell herself to pull away, but her hand only rested on his chest.

"Believe in yourself. You have more strength and power than you realize." His light touch trailed into her throat, petting gently, like he was stroking a kitten, coaxing it to purr.

More waves of sensation rippled into her, making her feel prickly and filling her with yearning.

What was he doing to her? She searched his eyes, but her gaze was drawn to his mouth. So stern, but looking as smooth as the rose petals had been. Would they feel the same against her own?

She unconsciously rolled her lips inward, dampening them with the tip of her tongue before she parted them to draw a breath of anticipation.

There was a flash behind his eyes that should have alarmed her, but it only sparked a flame of excitement.

"Do you want me to kiss you?" His voice was a rumble against the hand still on his chest. Was his heart thumping faster beneath her palm?

"Yes." The word came from the depths of her lungs, without any logic attached. As his head dipped, she closed her eyes.

His mouth settled on hers lightly at first, as though he was giving her time to become accustomed to the wild buzzing that filled her lips. No. His mouth was not the cool softness of the rose. It was hot and damp. He slowly deepened the kiss, releasing a growl of relish, as if she was something he'd been waiting for and he planned to savor every bite of her.

Her heart skipped with thrill. This was a kiss unlike any she'd experienced and she quit trying to analyze it because he was inciting an intoxicating rush that emptied her head. This wasn't sexual attraction, she realized distantly. It was sexual *hunger*.

It was visceral and consuming, driving her hands of their own accord to twine around his neck, hanging on because she grew dizzy while he cupped the back of her head and ravished her mouth with his own.

He wrapped his arm harder around her and her sore muscles protested, but there was comfort in the embrace, too. As if he was sheltering her even as he claimed her. It was the tight hold of a lover as he tipped them off a cliff together.

She pressed closer, savoring the ache. She was in danger of drowning all over again, but this time she had someone to hold on to. She wasn't alone.

They caught their breath and tilted their heads the other way. His teeth lightly scraped her bottom lip before his tongue soothed, then brushed against her own. His wide palm slid down to scald circles of heat across her bottom, sending heat spooling through her abdomen.

She arched closer and felt the thick, implacable shape of his arousal against her mound.

Startled, she drew back.

He kept hold of her, but loosely. His arms were still hard and unbreakable, but he was only steadying her while he looked at her through his thick lashes, expression inscrutable, yet satisfied.

"You're perfectly safe," he assured her. "But you didn't imagine you weren't having an effect on me, did you?" His thumb stroked her upper arm.

She swallowed, utterly disconcerted by that effect.

"I'm not averse to something more personal

developing between us, but we'll talk about that after we've dealt with Francois." He slid his hand down her hair again. This time it was a deliberate caress that ended with him pressing her hair into the side of her neck.

Words of protest backed up in her throat, making it hard to breathe.

"Shall we go?" He dropped his hand to catch at hers. He led her back into the labyrinth.

"Is there no shortcut out of this?" she asked plaintively.

"Wouldn't that be nice?" He sounded amused. "But such is life. We're trapped inside the one we're given. It's a pleasant change to have company, though," he added dryly, keeping hold of her hand as he drew her along the twisting paths.

CHAPTER FOUR

As MUCH AS Felipe enjoyed sex, he rarely took lovers. They always seemed to be poisoned by Francois, either working for his brother, or soon turned away by the blood sport between the twins.

Of the relationships he'd had, however, he had never been impaled by such a searing and immediate desire for anyone.

This haze of lust was as dangerous as any haze of rage might be, he cautioned himself. He ought to be taking their kiss as the warning of an uncontrolled burn that it was, but he spent the walk to the guest wing mentally recollecting the melting of her curves against his front, her soft gasp as they barely stopped for air, and the lovely shape of her bottom filling his palm.

That well of sensuality within her was a delightful discovery that teased him to hurry with his machinations against his brother, but now that she had agreed to move against Francois, Felipe wouldn't rush her on any level. Each domino would be placed with precision so they would topple in succession, at exactly the right time. Once it was done, he would have all the time in the world for her. *Them*.

"What—?" She halted as he drew her into a bedroom. She yanked her hand free of his and glared at him with betrayal.

"I brought you here to sleep." He waved at the wide, canopied bed with the royal crest on its silk coverlet.

She continued to look skeptical.

"When you wake, explore the castle, but stay inside. In fact, I'd like you to visit the infirmary to have your injuries looked at. If you want fresh clothes, the maids will bring you something from my closet."

"Why don't I wear something of theirs?" she asked with a confused frown.

"None are tall enough. And you are not part of my housekeeping staff, Claudine. On the contrary, you are extremely valuable to me. I want my staff to know that." He peeled down the blankets on the bed.

She stood unmoving, a mutinous pout on her lips.

Her eyes were so bruised with tiredness he wanted to pick her up and put her in the bed himself, but he had to reinforce this tentative trust between them. What he hadn't expected was that he would have to trust her to look after herself and go to sleep.

His concern for her was a new color for him. As a future ruler, he was invested in the well-being of his subjects, but in a very broad way. On a micro level, he'd always been forced to look after his own interests because no one else had. His inner circle was trustworthy enough that he valued them and would attempt to help any who suffered a health crisis or other tragedy, but they were all replaceable. He didn't *worry* about them.

He was worried about her, though. Mostly because he had a pressing engagement and had to leave her here. That wasn't sitting well with him at all, but it couldn't be helped.

"I'll see you later." He made himself leave and close the door behind himself. "Help her find the infirmary when she rises," he told the guard who had taken a position at the door. "Allow her to go anywhere she likes within the castle walls."

"Yes, sir." He managed to hide the bulk of his surprise, but Felipe understood they were all baffled as to why he was showing so much deference to one of his brother's contestants.

"Your Highness." His private secretary, Vinicio, rose from a nearby chair, ever-present tablet clasped in his hand. "Your meeting with the King is still on schedule?"

"Yes." Felipe's father had messaged last night.

Felipe hated to leave Claudine alone for even an hour, but it would allow him to learn very quickly if she intended to betray him. Also, canceling a meeting with the King would be highly suspicious. Rather than tip his cards, he would continue as if nothing untoward had happened here. "We'll take the helicopter."

There was a boat moored on the lee side of the island, but it sat in a lift next to the wharf to protect it from the constant battering of shifting seas. He often used it on fine days like today, but he was running late.

On his way out, he told his head of security, "I'll be at the palace for an hour. If anything happens to our guest while I'm gone, you are the first one I'll kill." He said it lightly, but he wasn't joking, not really.

The man swallowed. "For anything to happen, I would have to be dead."

Felipe nodded his satisfaction with that answer.

"Send two guards with me. The rest can stay here." He didn't expect trouble, but better safe than sorry.

Fifteen minutes later, he was descending to the palace grounds. Francois's red cabriolet was zipping through the palace gates at the same time. How tiresome. He had hoped this was crown business.

Both Felipe and Francois had apartments here

in the royal palace, but the day Felipe had broken Francois's nose was the day Felipe had moved to Sentinella. It was less convenient than living on the main island, but Sentinella did what it was designed to do and held the world—and his brother—at bay.

Francois stayed in his beach villa when he was in Nazarine, but mostly traveled the globe from film festivals to raves to solar eclipse parties, all under his portfolio of "economic development."

They arrived in the upper gallery at the same time from different directions. Felipe acknowledged his twin with a curt nod. Francois curled his lip at him, but said nothing.

Their father's private secretary greeted them and showed them to their parents' parlor.

Family business, then. Otherwise, the King would meet with them in his office.

They entered what might pass for a living room in other people's homes. The furniture made an effort toward comfort over ostentatious style, but there were still plenty of relics that provided as much forgiveness as a church pew.

Queen Paloma wore one of her exquisitely tailored skirt suits, but only minimal jewelry and no hat. She sat on the edge of a sofa cushion, expression somber. She looked up as Felipe came through, nodded politely, then brightened when Francois came in behind him.

"Padre," Felipe acknowledged King Enzo even though his father didn't turn from his contemplation out the window.

"Mamma." Felipe kissed the cheeks his mother offered.

"Cucciolo," she said with affection directed at Francois. "How are your girls this year?"

Girls. Not women. Felipe's conscience gave another twist that he had ignored the pageant for so long, rather than seeing it for what it was.

"Belissima," Francois claimed. "It will be impossible to find the winner."

Felipe bit back a caustic *Oh, I found her.*

"Sit with me." The Queen kept hold of Francois's hand.

"What's wrong, Mamma?" Francois settled beside her, his demeanor one of fawning consolation.

Felipe averted his gaze so he wouldn't vomit with disgust.

The Queen said nothing. The King kept his stiff back turned toward them.

This was bad, Felipe understood. The silence went on long enough to grow a layer of dust before King Enzo finally turned.

"I am unwell. Critically unwell. Pancreatic cancer," he stated. "They've given me a year."

Another silence crashed down on the room.

"How did they not find it sooner?" Felipe asked.

"I felt fine until recently. I will require surgery

and other treatments. You'll assume more of my duties, beginning immediately." He sent that order to Felipe with a bracing stare.

"Of course." They were not a sentimental family. Felipe kept a neutral expression on his face as he inquired, "Shall I cancel my meetings in New York?"

"No. For now, this news stays in this room. Everything must appear normal."

"Normal" was being flipped inside out, Felipe thought dourly. He could feel Francois already scheming to turn this to his advantage.

"There will be no more of your faffing about, taking your time in marrying and producing an heir," the King threw at Felipe. "I want to know the throne is secured. Do not make me look at other alternatives."

And there it was, the one twisted pathway Francois had to gaining an upper hand over him. On more than one occasion, Francois had tried to persuade their father to overturn the law of succession. They were twins born within minutes, virtually at the same time. Surely, Francois often argued, he had exactly as much right to the throne as Felipe?

Faced with such a lengthy and complex legal process, King Enzo had never given the request serious attention, but the way he held Felipe's gaze right now was an overt dare.

Felipe wanted to believe his father was bluffing. Given how little time Enzo had left, Felipe doubted he could go through with his threat, but the fact he would level such a stark warning had Felipe's mind cycling through the handful of women he had considered over the years as a potential wife. None had ever appealed strongly enough that he could imagine spending a lifetime with her.

None had sparked a sexual craving in him like the one that had roared to life in him a few hours ago.

"Competition has always worked well to motivate the pair of you," his father continued. "Therefore, I lift my embargo on your marrying before Felipe," he said to Francois. "I want to see the next generation before I die. But those children must be legitimate. Marry first, then make our next ruler." He directed that at both of them.

"Time to break out your short list, Mamma." Francois patted the back of the hand he held. An avid light had come into his eyes. He genuinely saw a chance to leapfrog himself onto the throne.

The Queen started to smile conspiratorially, then straightened her features and looked to her other son.

"You've already seen it," she reminded Felipe in a cool tone. "I'm not sure if you've selected anyone from it, though…?"

"Oh, yes. The firstborn must have first pick." Francois asked with mock deference, "Are there any candidates you consider off-limits to me?"

On principle, all of them, but when it came down to it, one in particular.

Felipe was still highly skeptical his father would go through with deposing him in favor of Francois, but he couldn't allow Francois to entertain the belief that he had a shot at the crown. Every inch was a mile to Francois.

No, Felipe had to marry promptly and beget his successor.

"Any woman who is willing to have you is yours to court. I have someone else in mind," Felipe said.

"Oh?" Francois narrowed his eyes while their mother blinked in surprise.

"Oh?" their father asked in a tone that demanded more information.

It was an impulsive declaration, one that was also cold and calculated, but Felipe had learned to trust his instincts.

Right now, all his instincts said, *Claudine.*

Claudine woke feeling significantly better.

Her laundered underthings had been delivered along with refreshments and a selection of clothing from—presumably—Felipe's closet.

She rolled up the cuffs of his pin-striped shirt

to expose her wrists and tied the tails of it at her waist. His gray trousers needed cinching with a braided leather belt that allowed the tongue to go in anywhere. Once she had tied her hair back with a handkerchief, she felt almost like her old self.

Then she stepped out of her room and remembered she was still a very long way from "normal."

"The Prince asked me to show you to the infirmary," the guard said. "Please follow me."

The Prince. The one who had asked if she wanted him to kiss her, then had swept away every thought in her head. His kiss had broken a spell she hadn't known she was under. She wasn't a particularly passionate person. Or hadn't been. Not before he had awakened her senses and lit fires of bright, physical yearnings inside her.

I'm not averse to something more personal developing between us...

He had cast a spell with that same kiss, making her think that she wanted something intimate with him. That she was capable of matching him in that way.

You have more strength and power than you realize.

She didn't, though! They occupied very different stratospheres and that was only the beginning of their inequalities. He was simply too much in every way. Too masculine, too powerful, too hard.

Too hot. She might be pretty, but he radiated the raw beauty of lightning and hurricanes and comets crashing into planets.

He had probably meant she was powerful in terms of the damage she could do to his brother. In that respect, she felt like a pawn, one that Felipe was willing to sacrifice for his own ends.

No, she was susceptible to him because he was an accomplished seducer. Anything "more personal" would be pure self-destruction, so she would steer clear of it.

The doctor pronounced she was "healing nicely," cautioned her to keep her fluids up and gave her another headache tablet for her various aches.

From there, she wandered the gallery, taking in the sculptures and paintings of former rulers— how strange to realize she wasn't in a museum. This was the Prince's family album.

Amused by that thought, she turned down a hallway dedicated to portraits of one bygone queen in particular, shown with her many children at different ages. She looked…defiant?

Claudine found herself studying the one where she sat behind her husband, her hand resting on his shoulder. Claudine looked into the eyes of that hard-faced man, searching for some sign of Felipe or Francois, but they seemed to have inherited their looks from her, not him.

Yes. Felipe might not have anything feminine about him, but he had this Queen's same unflinching stare and enigmatic expression.

"Here you are," Felipe said.

She nearly leaped out of her skin, gasping and clutching at her heart as though she'd been caught with the family jewels in her hands.

"You didn't hear the helicopter return?" he asked with amusement, coming to stand beside her. "Or my voice just now, asking where to find you?"

"No." She rubbed the goose bumps from her arms as she sent a wary look at him.

Felipe studied the image of the woman looking down on them.

"Giulia. My father's grandmother. She was held here on the island. Did you know that?"

"No." Claudine had read a little of the kingdom's history, but had mostly researched its pop culture and trends, finding that was the best way to bring an audience onto her side.

"Sentinella's isolation makes a perfect holding cell. Pirates stored gold here at different times. That booty was claimed by my ancestors when they took possession of the rest of the islands." He quirked his mouth as he glanced at her. "The sailors in our navies were always very loyal while stationed here, since the alternative was a longer swim than yours last night. For a time, it was a monastery. The monks built the labyrinth. Then my great-great-grandfather kicked them out when he ensconced Giulia here." He nodded at the Queen. "She was not warming to their arranged marriage. He kept her here until she had given him two sons. They didn't arrive right away. She bore him four daughters as well." He pointed at the portrait of the Queen with all six of her children. "She was here for twenty years."

"That's awful."

Some unspoken light of knowledge entered his eyes. It was the same one from the portrait. "Let me show you her library."

Her body prickled with awareness of danger as she followed him, but it wasn't fear or dread. It was that other danger that made her nostrils sting while all the cells in her body seemed to swivel and align themselves to an awareness of him. Some involuntary part of her insisted on calling out to him.

She tried to tamp it down as she moved past him through the door he opened and entered the sort of room she'd only seen in movies. It was three stories of shelved books accessed by flights of stairs and narrow, railed galleries, and rolling ladders. There were reading nooks built beneath tall windows and big, comfortable chairs by the fire and a desk with inkpots and candleholders.

"This answers the question, 'How did people

survive before streaming services?'" she murmured, trying to imagine how much time one would need to read all of these. "You're saying this castle isn't a dungeon? She had all this? It was still cruel to keep her here, don't you think?"

"It was," he agreed with a nod. "She was not a woman who submitted to confinement without a fight, though. She wrote here." He pointed to the desk. "Subversive, disruptive messages about rights that women still fight for today. She wrote her beliefs in many of these books, so many that her husband couldn't find and destroy all of them unless he burned the entire library to the ground. She smuggled her writings off the island in various ways—often using her children and maids. They were published at different times, humiliating the King. When he finally said she could join him on Stella Vista, she insisted on staying here another three years, purely as a show of resistance. Eventually, she took her place beside him, mostly for the sake of her children. He was well known to have a mistress by then, so they had little to do with one another outside of their royal duties."

"That's so sad."

"Do you think so? I find her inspiring." He moved along a row of books, seeming to look for a particular title. He started to withdraw it, then left it stuck out halfway. A few books along, he pushed three inward an inch. "She found a way to assert herself despite the strictures of her life. She didn't choose to be born a princess, and she didn't choose to be married off to a king, but she found ways to live the life she was given on her own terms."

"Is that how you feel?" She was taken by how the sunlight fell through the window onto him, allowing her to see him perhaps more clearly than she had before. "Are you trapped in a life you didn't ask for?"

"Not trapped, precisely. I have more agency than she did and there's a great deal of privilege that comes with my wealth and title," he said with pithy self-deprecation. "But there are times when I feel cornered into a particular situation or action."

He was working his way back along the shelf, doing the same thing to the row of books above the first, shifting some in, drawing some out so the spine was on the edge of the shelf. It looked like piano keys being played by a ghost.

"Do you do that to remind the staff to dust them?" she asked.

"No, they don't know about this." He reached the end and pressed into the bulk of the shelf. There was an audible ping, like a loud spring. An entire section of shelf next to the ones he'd been rearranging now swung open like a door.

"A secret passage?" she whispered in awe.

"Down to where the monks made their wine.

It has an external entrance near the wharf where the supply ships docked. Queen Giulia would lock herself into her library to read, then slip down those stairs to let her lover in below."

"Who was he?" Claudine couldn't help inching closer to peer into the dark well of the stairs, catching a scent of cool, dank air.

"According to her diary, there were many. A captain, a guard, a sailor. Her children were conceived in this room, not her marriage bed. When she thought she might be pregnant, she would write to the King and insist he visit her."

"Did he know?" she asked with hushed astonishment.

"He must have suspected, given the fact that all of his children favored their mother and didn't look much like each other or him, but no one speaks of it. I learned the truth when I chose to make Sentinella my home. I hired a librarian to catalog the books and they found her stash of journals. One explains how she commissioned the shelf to hide the passageway and bribed the journeyman with sexual favors to take that secret to his grave. He would have been executed if he had admitted to touching a queen, so…" He shrugged.

"Why on earth are you telling *me*? This isn't just a family secret. You're saying your family doesn't belong on the throne!"

"The throne was stolen from her family, not

his. Giulia was the sacrificial lamb married to her family's conqueror to appease the masses so they wouldn't revolt."

"That still doesn't explain why you would tell *me*." How was she supposed to carry such explosive knowledge?

"I thought you would find it interesting. And I want you to have a sense of who we are as a family and what we'll do for the sake of the throne. What we'll do to keep the right person on the throne." He closed the shelf and moved along, straightening all the books again. "I want you to understand that you have choices, even when it might seem as though you don't. Most of all, I need you to trust me. That means I have to trust you."

"I trust you." A little. Her voice didn't even convince herself. It caused him to send her a disparaging glance.

"When we were fifteen, our father made it clear that he would not recognize an illegitimate child from either of us. Nor would he accept Francois marrying before I have a wife and an heir." He grabbed the edge of the shelf to give it a firm pull, checking it was closed securely. It remained firmly in place.

He brushed his hands together, then looked at her in a way that made her wilt on the inside. Fear? Premonition of some kind. He wasn't a man who told stories and revealed secrets without expecting something in return. Something big. Something of equal weight.

"Are you toying with him? Why haven't you married?" she asked.

"He does everything he can to stop me. It's both spite and strategy. If I have children, he is pushed down the line of succession so he tells women that I'm a brute with a temper, one who encourages our father to hold Nazarine back from the modern world so our people are easier to control. He tells them I have our country's parliament in my pocketbook. Or he keeps *them* in *his* pocketbook. That's what happened with my first fiancée. The second one couldn't take all this animosity and palace intrigue. I didn't blame her for breaking it off. It was better to know early that she didn't have the stomach for it."

"But not *every* woman would be turned off by that!" He was a prince destined to be a king, for heaven's sake.

"True, but I'm cynical when it comes to women and relationships. And I've always felt as though I had plenty of time. Until today." He became unnervingly somber. "For reasons I can't share with you at this time, our father lifted his embargo on Francois marrying and producing an heir before me."

"Oh?" That strange sting on her arms was her

own fingernails digging into her skin. Her ears were ringing, her breath backing up in her lungs. She didn't know why she had suddenly grown so tense, but she was hanging on his every word.

"Obviously, any child Francois produced would be superseded by any of mine that came along after, but that would be messy. If Francois were the father of a future ruler, even for a brief period, he would capitalize on all the power that would come with such a position. He would fiercely resist my child taking its rightful place. Rather than put Nazarine through countless, pointless battles of succession, I must marry immediately and do my best to procreate before he does."

He looked straight at her. Into her. She had the sensation that her heart was falling down a flight of stairs and he was watching it happen.

"I don't understand," she said carefully.

"Of course, you do. You know exactly where I'm headed because you're very smart, Claudine. It's one of the things that attracts me to you."

"No. It— I— *No.*" Her ears were ringing. "You can't be serious, Felipe. *No.*"

"I am very serious, Claudine. I want you to marry me."

CHAPTER FIVE

"You don't even know me." Claudine shook her head, trying to convince herself she'd misheard him. "I don't know you. No. I can't."

"Listen to what I'm offering. I've looked into your mother's condition—"

"Don't you dare threaten my mother!"

"This is not a threat, Claudine. It's bribery. *Listen.* There are a number of excellent clinics, some in the US, some in Europe. She'll have a full assessment and any treatment she feels is right for her."

"*Please* do not talk as if I've already agreed to this mad plan."

"Believe it or not, your reluctance only reassures me that you're not an agent for Francois, or an opportunist. My greatest hurdle to marriage has always been the struggle to find a bride I can trust, one who cannot be influenced by him. That's you."

"Believe it or not—" she barely kept her tone

this side of strident "—your demand that I marry you less than twenty-four hours after we met does *not* reassure *me*. Nothing about this does."

She started toward the door, but stopped at the desk, then turned back to him.

"Here is what I'm willing to do." She fought to maintain a calm voice. "I'll write down every detail I can recollect from the time they told us where we were going last night until I washed up on your beach. I will give you that in exchange for a flight home. You can use my statement however you like. Surely that's enough to slow your brother down?"

"From finding a wife? Not every woman is as discerning as you are. Francois will find someone very quickly," he said pithily. "When you're ready to release a statement, we'll find a way to do it so it impacts you as little as possible. I will protect you to the best of my ability once it's out there, but think about it, Claudine. The best protection for *you* will be as the fiancée of a future king. Look at this fortress around you." He waved his arms.

"These walls don't protect me from public opinion! People will think it's a stunt. Is it? It is! Your family wouldn't allow you to marry *me*. You're trying to use me to make some kind of point."

"When it comes to marriage, you possess the *only* quality that matters to me. You hate my brother as much as I do. You are the one I want to marry and my parents will have to accept you."

"Listen to yourself! You want to base a marriage on hatred? You want to bring children into— I don't even know if I can have children. Do you realize that? I've never tried."

"Is there some reason to believe you can't?"

"No. Not that it's any of your business," she added hotly, then clutched the sides of her head. "I can't believe we're even having this conversation. *Please* send me home."

"Time is of the essence, Claudine. Otherwise, I would woo you."

She strangled on a laugh of disbelief.

"I am very capable of seduction," he said coolly. "Which I will demonstrate at the appropriate time."

That was both terrifying and intriguing. He came to loom beside her, forcing her into taking a faltering step backward.

"For now, yes. It's a good idea for you to record exactly what happened the other night." He opened a drawer in the desk and set out sheets of linen paper with a pen that appeared to be wrought from 24 karat gold. "I'll speak to you after I've checked on a few things."

Felipe was operating on the assumption that Claudine would marry him. He could trust her more than anyone else he'd ever considered tying himself to and he had no other immediate option. Finding a way to convince her was a small detail among many as far as executing his plan went, but he didn't abandon good sense altogether.

He went back to the dossier Vinicio had hurriedly prepared shortly after her arrival, wanting to ensure there wouldn't be any unpleasant surprises in her background.

Claudine's history of entering pageants would be seen as questionable, particularly by his mother. An American beauty contestant was not who she had in mind for either of her sons, especially the one whose wife would usurp her own title.

On the other hand, Claudine wouldn't have consistently won those contests if she had had a history of gambling debts or sexual exploits. Her image was wholesome yet progressive, given she had been born to a pair of women.

Queen Paloma wouldn't have any prejudice against Claudine being the child of a same-sex marriage. Nazarine had been at the forefront of adopting recognition of those unions, but Claudine was solidly middle-class, not even an heiress to a tech billionaire or some other nouveau riche family that the Queen might force herself to accept into the fold.

Her pageants meant she was well-traveled. Her on-camera demeanor was always polished and composed, her responses to questions well-constructed and intelligent, if brief and idealistic. She spoke fondly of a childhood dog and developed new talents for each pageant. She could write calligraphy, shoot an arrow into a bull's-eye, recognize birdsongs and perform rhythmic dance.

A wife with valuable connections would be useful, given Felipe would be taking on even more diplomatic and economic duties as his father's health declined.

Something like regret panged through him. He knew he ought to feel more than that. Vinicio had taken a month off work when he'd lost his father and he'd been a different man when he returned. Not openly morose, but somber. Felipe had accidentally overheard him comforting his mother on a call once and they'd both been crying.

The idea of being emotionally broken by his father's illness was a foreign concept to Felipe. Their relationship had always been defined by their roles. His father had drawn a hard line between his two sons early on, brutally severing Felipe from a connection to his twin. The closest Felipe had ever come to experiencing parental doting was witnessing the Queen showering it upon Francois.

He could see now why his father had given him nothing but a dispassionate visage, though. Felipe's detachment from his father's illness would allow him to continue acting in the best interests of his country while their family dealt with the loss.

Nazarine had small but reliable agricultural and manufacturing sectors. Their location on a trade route in the Mediterranean made Stella Vista's main port an important service and transfer facility for shipping companies. Tourism was also a heavy economic driver, which was why losing the pageant could be a blow to hotels and other service industries.

Nazarine had always had an excellent reputation for its boatyards and shipbuilders, too. Felipe had been pressing for the development of specialized higher education programs—marine architecture and the newer marine information technologies. That was what his trip to New York was about and he looked forward to advancing that.

Claudine's citizenship wouldn't hurt him there.

No, the more he thought about it, the more he saw she was a perfect fit as his queen.

Literally. Did his determination to wed her have anything to do with this lust he was nursing? Hell, yes, it did. He was trying to ignore it, but merely coming upon her in the hall had sparked rampant fantasies. Perhaps it had been seeing her in his own clothes, as though she'd picked them up from his floor after he'd ravished her. He'd found himself dreaming of loosening those clothes and taking her against the wall or sprawling naked with her beneath the eyes of his ancestors.

He shook off those distracting fantasies and sought out Vinicio.

"How is the pageant reacting to Claudine's disappearance?" Felipe asked.

"Acute, but well-muffled panic. Some contestants were told she missed the photo shoot due to food poisoning. Others heard she had a family emergency. The police are quietly reviewing security footage, trying to determine if and when she came back from the cruise and whether she returned to the hotel. One of the Prince's minions has asked a few of the contestants whether she seemed drunk at the party."

"Setting it up to claim she fell into the water of her own clumsy accord," Felipe said with disgust.

"Prince Francois was not visible at the photo shoot, either."

"He was at the palace," Felipe reminded Vinicio.

"He then went into unscheduled meetings with the pageant organizers. It seems likely they were discussing Ms. Bergqvist."

"Perhaps." Francois would be looking for a way to wrap up her disappearance as quickly as possible because he had a new goal. Felipe explained that his brother would quickly become occupied with finding a wife. "He might even shut down future pageants himself, if he's about to become a married man."

Felipe rose to pace off his restlessness.

"May I ask, sir, if you are also—"

"Claudine will be my wife," he stated.

"Very good, sir." Vinicio nodded. "Congratulations."

"Thank you. You have a lot of work ahead of you. Let's hammer out a timeline beginning with my taking her to the palace to introduce her to my parents."

"Claudine."

He startled her again, but not as violently this time. She had been waiting for him, her statement folded in her hand while she stared out the window at the hazy shape of Stella Vista, measuring the distance between agency and responsibility. Between doing what was right for her and what was right for other women, and her mother, and the greater good.

Writing out her statement had forced her to see all the small ways that Francois had manipulated her. He was a truly terrible person who had to be stopped from preying on women, but also from preying on his brother and his country.

Was she really the woman to do it, though?

Surely there were other ways Felipe could keep his twin from taking the throne?

She turned and smiled faintly as she brought him the pages.

"Thank you," he said solemnly, but didn't open the document to read what she'd written. Instead, he lifted his gaze to let it travel over her in a way that was both rueful and admiring. "I like seeing you in my clothing."

"Why?"

"Why does any man want to put a ring on a woman? To claim her, of course."

Her heart lurched, but even as she said, "That's very barbaric," there was a primitive part of her that responded to his possessiveness.

Did he know? Was that why that air of ironic amusement came over his expression?

"So…um…now that I've kept my side of the bargain…" She waved at the pages he held.

"Did you think my acceptance of this was an agreement?" He set the pages on the edge of the desk.

"Seriously?" she huffed. "You can't expect me to marry a per—a complete stranger!"

"I've shared some very personal details with you," he said with a hint of indignance. "More than I've ever offered to anyone. What else would you like to know? I prefer cats to dogs. They're more self-sufficient. I don't have a favorite color because I have the type of color blindness that sees red and green as the same shade. I am not close with my family," he finished facetiously.

She wanted to toss back something equally sarcastic, but she was realizing they actually had shared quite a lot of deeply personal things. It wasn't enough to base a marriage on, though. Was it?

"I prefer dogs," she informed him coolly. "For the unconditional love they offer. Which, coincidentally, is what I would look for in a husband."

He gave a small snort of disappointment. "Love is not a requirement for a successful union. It's a detriment to getting what you really want and need from life."

"No, it's not!" She stared at him, astonished. "It *is* what everyone needs from life."

"How?"

"What do you mean, *how*?"

"You can't eat it. You can't breathe it. I have never experienced it yet I am alive, so how can you say it's a necessity of life?"

"Because—" She faltered, startled by the way he had said that so blithely. He had never experienced love. Never? Really?

"No need for pity," he said sardonically. "I don't miss it."

"You must. Have you really never had anyone

love you?" she argued. "It's companionship and—and—loyalty, and caring—"

"You really do want a dog."

"Love is offering respect and affection and emotional support to someone you feel great esteem toward," she insisted hotly. "Have you never felt any of that?"

"Have you?" he challenged. "Are you in love with someone right now?"

"No," she admitted sullenly. That was why she couldn't describe it without stammering. She'd been dismissed as a gangly, ugly duckling as a child, then treated as a sex object once she began developing curves. It had been an overnight transformation that she was still trying to reckon with.

"No," he repeated, as if she had confirmed some crime-proving detail in a cross-examination. "Because those feelings you're describing do not magically fuse into something bigger than the sum of their parts. If you want to call loyalty and respect and sexual attraction 'love,' have at it, but it is not an emotion unto itself. It's certainly not a necessity to anyone."

"I've never heard anything so cynical in my life." She could only stare at him, agog. Disappointed. "Did one of your fiancées hurt you? How did you become like this?"

"I grew up," he said flatly.

She physically recoiled from that. "Possessing a heart is immature?"

"Believing that some imaginary manifestation of a heart must be proffered and accepted before a marital relationship can move forward is immature, yes."

"Do you even hear what a cold, empty offer this is that you're making me? You should have left me to die on the beach." She flung out a hand in that vague direction.

"Is this really an obstacle for you?" Impatience edged into his tone. "You're worried that marrying me will keep you from drowning in sentiment over some nameless person you haven't even met yet? If he is out there, why hasn't he come to save you? What will he offer you when he does? Pretty words? Will they complete you in some way that you are deficient in right now? I see you as a whole person exactly as you are. You don't need anyone to prop you up emotionally."

"You don't know that." On the inside she was Swiss cheese, nothing but holes. She suspected it was caused by the loss of her mother at such a young age, but she had suffered this sense of missing pieces of herself for a long time. The pageants hadn't helped. They skewed her self-image into only focusing on the external view of herself. Who was she beneath the superficial surface?

Who did she want to be? A nurse? A teacher? Swedish? American?

"If you lack the confidence to recognize your own mental strength, I will build that up along with providing anything else that you lack. Including a dog, if you insist."

"Now you're just mocking me." She folded her arms. "It's not immature for me to want to marry someone who *cares* about me."

"To what degree? I care about you enough not to leave you half-dead on a beach. I care about how this—" he tapped next to the pages she had written "—will play out and affect you. You have to stop thinking of marriage in the terms that were sold to you by greeting cards and ads for diamond rings. I'm hiring you for a position, Claudine. You've devoted yourself to pageants as a career, have you not? Those organizers ask you to uphold a certain image and discourage you from having relationships that could cast you in an unflattering light, no? They tell you what to eat and where to stand and you are compensated accordingly. This is much the same."

"The position you're trying to fill is sex work and surrogacy."

"I plan to do the work, *cara mia*," he shot back. "The sex will be all pleasure on your side. Our kiss earlier was a promise on that front, was it not?" The flare of light behind his eyes dared her to deny it.

Her voice stalled in her throat. She blushed and looked away.

The sheer power he radiated made her quiver deep inside, in a place that was frighteningly vulnerable. At the same time, there was a craving in her, a pull. It was edged with the most primal needs she possessed. She wanted to be closer to that force. To him. She wanted his touch on her, his lips. Him.

"I was under the impression you wanted children," he said gruffly. "Am I wrong?"

"I do," she admitted huskily. It was part of that blank space in her life. Neither of her mothers had family and her surviving mother was facing a life that could be cut short if she didn't receive the help she needed. Claudine's only other family connection was that nascent one to a man who had twice walked into a clinic.

Or she could make a family of her own.

"You're asking me to accept a life sentence in a loveless marriage," she said, torn between her mother's future and her own. "How is that different from the way Queen Giulia was imprisoned here?"

His cheek ticked.

"Five years, then," he said after a moment of thought, teeth gritted. "Give me five years of honest effort at conceiving at least two children. If you wish to divorce and look for your soul mate after that, we can do so. I'll ensure you have a home and everything you need for a good life here."

For some perverse reason, she found his willingness to get divorced very disappointing.

"What about our children? Would I have custody after that?"

"They will have to be raised here in Nazarine, but they will always be our children. Not mine. Not yours. *Ours*. You will have as much influence over their upbringing as I do."

All her objections to this bizarre suggestion of his were being neatly removed.

In casting for another reason to refuse him, her gaze snagged on the pages she'd written. She had offered that to him with supreme dread of the ordeal it promised, but she hadn't seen any other way to get herself home.

"What about…?" She nodded at the papers.

"It remains your decision if and when to come forward. I will absolutely protect you to the best of my ability when you do. In the short term, it's a powerful bargaining chip with my father." He picked up the papers and tapped their folded edge on the table. "To ensure he approves our marriage."

Her heart gave a swoop in her chest. "I—" Was she agreeing to this?

"I'm offering you the care your mother needs and a good life for you and your children. As an added bonus, you will have bested my brother in a way that he could not have foreseen when he thought he could assault you without consequence."

His grim tone made her catch her breath. He really was the darker prince.

He had to be, she realized with a chill in her heart. Otherwise, he would have lost to Francois long ago.

No. Not darker. Harder. He wore a sheen of titanium armor. What he had said about never experiencing love kept echoing in her ears. In her chest. What would that do to a person except force them to form an impermeable shell?

Let me in, she couldn't help thinking.

Foolish. She knew that. There was no changing someone who didn't want to be changed.

Would she want him to change, though? She was enthralled with him exactly as he was.

"There's no one else I can trust the way I can trust you, Claudine," he urged in a low voice. "You're not giving up power by agreeing. You're exercising the power you have in this moment."

Really? Because she felt weak. She felt as though she was capitulating to something inside herself that had nothing to do with personal agency and everything to do with wanting to be near him. To know him.

If she walked away now, she would go back to that blurry version of herself. She would never know who she could have become if he was in her life.

The one thing she did know about herself was that she wasn't a coward. She didn't shy from something simply because it looked difficult.

She bit her lips and nodded. "Yes. I'll marry you."

CHAPTER SIX

IT WASN'T MUCH of an exaggeration to say Claudine's life changed in an instant.

The fact was, it had already changed when she had leaped from the speedboat to swim away from her life as a pageant contestant, but she could have gone back to her old life from there. It would have been altered and she would have faced challenges, but she wouldn't have given her life *to* someone else.

That was how she felt as Felipe whisked her under cover of darkness to the royal palace on Stella Vista.

By then, she had spoken briefly to her mother, who was now ensconced in a private and well-secured clinic for protection against paparazzi and anyone else who might try to reach her. They were planning to visit her after they announced their engagement.

"You'll meet my parents in the morning," Felipe said as he showed her into a private apartment.

"Relax, eat. Ask Vinicio for anything you need. Speak to no one but the staff in these rooms."

Did she feel guarded by Vinicio? Yes, but she soon realized this wasn't any apartment. It was Felipe's personal wing. The luxurious space was neat as a pin and included a small, well-stocked kitchen along with a breakfast room, a parlor, an office, a private terrace and a massive bedroom.

She perused the handful of photos on the walls. They showed Felipe in his youth, before he had been scarred, when he was still capable of smiling, and later, when that line on his face seemed to harden the rest of his features into its current hostile expression.

There were no photos of his brother.

She pressed her fist to the knot in her middle and turned on the television. It was set to a news channel and the broadcaster spoke in Italian. Market numbers ran along the bottom.

"I don't think that's a good idea, *signorina*." Vinicio materialized before her.

"Why not?"

"The coverage of your disappearance is unflattering."

"To *me*?" She pointed at herself, astonished.

"*Sì*. Prince Felipe is allowing it for the moment to maintain the illusion you are missing, but you may find it upsetting." He turned off the television. "Perhaps we could run you a bath? Ippolita?" He moved into the bedroom that Claudine had only peered into.

A maid emerged from a dressing room. The pair exchanged some words in Italian.

The young woman smiled and nodded, then went back into the dressing room.

"Ippolita doesn't speak English, but she's been with us for some time and is fully vetted. Prince Felipe asked her to see what she could find for you at the local boutiques."

"Oh?" Claudine leaned to see into the dressing room where the young woman had been hanging gowns and women's clothing alongside shirts and suits.

"You'll be flying to Paris after your engagement announcement," Vinicio continued. "I've arranged for designers from Milan, New York and Tokyo to meet you there. You'll soon have abundant styles to choose from."

Claudine could hardly keep her jaw from dropping to the floor. She often wore designer clothing for the pageants, invariably on loan and always with great trepidation, given their value.

Ippolita reverently drew a peignoir off a hanger and presented it in a drape across her arms, anxiously searching Claudine's face for approval. It was almost too pretty to consider wearing with its lilac-colored satin and oyster gray lace.

"It's beautiful." Claudine blushed slightly, wondering what Ippolita was implying by offering it, but the stunning quality of the piece had her reaching to turn over the small label attached with a loop of satin ribbon. "Local?"

Ippolita nodded.

Claudine had not won as many pageants as she had by not understanding how the game was played.

"You should include this designer with the rest," Claudine suggested to Vinicio. "Most contestants wear the big names because that's what we're offered." It was lucrative for the pageant to promote them and made it more likely for a contestant to be chosen as an ambassador for those products in future. "I find it wins hearts when I wear something made by a designer in the host country, even if it's only a neck scarf."

Vinicio gave a considering nod while Ippolita carried the peignoir into the bathroom and hung it on the back of the door. She stoppered the enormous tub and opened the taps.

The tub was set between marble columns and built into a platform with two steps leading up to it. The fixtures were gold, as were the ones on the nearby sinks. A steam shower took up the entirety of the opposite wall.

Ippolita withdrew a blue bottle from behind the mirror and opened it, offering it to Claudine to smell it.

When Claudine nodded her approval, Ippolita poured a generous amount of liquid into the water, releasing the aroma of lavender, geranium and bergamot as well as starting a froth of bubbles.

Claudine felt rather useless, especially when Ippolita lowered the lights and said, *"Vino, signorina?"*

"Per favore," Claudine mumbled as she followed Ippolita back to the main room. "Can you please tell her she doesn't need to wait on me like this?" she said to Vinicio.

"Are you displeased with her?" Vinicio glanced between them. "We'll begin a hiring process tomorrow for your personal staff—"

"No! I mean, she's lovely." Claudine realized then that Ippolita was auditioning for a job she very much wanted. "I only meant I'm not used to this. I'm feeling very spoiled."

"I'm confident that is how the Prince would want you to feel," Vinicio said with a nod.

He exchanged another few words with Ippolita, who relaxed and smiled shyly, then finished pouring the wine and carried it on a tray into the bathroom.

Claudine was soon cosseted in warm water and a fragrant mass of bubbles that caressed her skin. The lights were dim and the gentle notes from pastoral classical pieces trickled in from hidden speakers. She pinched herself, wondering if this was even real.

It became very real when Felipe let himself in!

She sputtered slightly on the sip of wine she was in the middle of taking and sank deeper into the crackling bubbles. "We need to talk about your habit of barging in on me when I'm in the bath or shower."

"I'm starting as I mean to go on," he said dryly, noting, "It smells good in here." He came to sit on the edge of the tub. His gaze seemed to penetrate past the thick snow of foam. "You're comfortable?"

Naked in front of him like this? Not really.

"Vinicio said the pageant is saying unflattering things about me."

"He told me you seemed upset to learn that. They're trying to cover their own negligence by throwing fault on you. It's driven by my brother. They will all look that much more foolish when it's revealed you were with me all along." He stole her glass and sipped from it. "The King has approved our marriage."

She didn't know what impacted her more, his words or the way his gaze seemed to slam into hers, knocking her deeper into the water.

"I told him our marriage does not buy your silence about what Francois did to you. You'll speak up if and when the time is right for you. I mean that. How much you say, to whom and when, is completely in your control."

"And he accepted that?" She numbly lifted her hand from the water to accept the glass he handed back.

"Not gracefully, but certain things can't be hidden." His penetrating gaze traveled the clouds of bubbles before he touched the edge of the scrape on her arm where she had removed the soaked bandage. "My father has always enjoyed the dogfight between his sons, but this was not an attack on me. You weren't mine yet."

He traced his fingertip from her elbow to her shoulder, where he picked up a damp tendril of hair that had fallen from her clip. He lifted it to curl the tail of it around her topknot.

"Now that you are, I told him that if he expects me to silence you to protect my brother, then he has not been paying attention to the kind of men he has created." His voice was lethal, his absorbed expression mesmerizing.

Her body reacted with shivers of hot and cold. Her muscles were frozen while her bones were melting.

"I still have much to do. Eat something. Sleep." He bent and touched his mouth to hers. "Tomorrow will be a busy day."

* * *

Claudine woke with a gasp, aware someone was in the room with her.

"It's me," Felipe said as he slipped into the other side of the bed. "Go back to sleep."

She turned onto her side to face him, only able to see the vague outline of his shape against the darkness. He sighed once and lay still, completely relaxed, as though he had willed himself to sleep and it was done.

This is my life now. This is what I'll do. I'll sleep with this man from now on.

She could hardly fathom it. And sex? For procreation, obviously, but he had stated it would be all pleasure for her.

Her hand unconsciously curled into the sheet. Despite some virginal wariness, she wasn't as apprehensive as she ought to be. In fact, her body heated with a flush of anticipation as she imagined the loom of his wide shoulders over her. How would the weight of his hips feel between her legs? Or the sensation of his strong thighs pushing hers apart? Would it hurt when his flesh thrust into her?

Her inner flesh clenched involuntarily, aching with longing.

"Do you want me to help you sleep?" he asked in a rumble that made her pulse skip.

"What?" she squeaked. "I thought you were asleep."

"How can I sleep when I can feel the pounding of your heart and hear the unevenness in your breath?"

She swallowed, mortified.

"I'm as aroused as you are, thinking of what it might be like when we make love." He shifted to sprawl his arm over his head, staying on his back. "But I came into this bed planning to show you that I won't act on my desires unless it's something you want as badly as I do. The only way this alliance will work is if we trust each other and here, where you're most vulnerable, is the most important place for me to build your trust."

He was aroused? Did he have the same throbbing ache in his pelvis that she did? If she reached out, would she find him as hard as he'd been when he had kissed her? Aside from a few fumbling caresses with fellow college students, she hadn't really explored a man. Even those had been driven more by curiosity than genuine desire.

This fire of yearning in her was a far more carnal want. She needed to know how hard he was. How thick. How hot and weighty against her palm. She wanted to *feel* him.

"I could very easily be persuaded to take the edge off your cravings with my fingers or my mouth. Would you like that?"

The rough texture of his voice might as well have been his tongue between her thighs, her response was such a visceral rush of damp heat into that place.

It wasn't rational! *This* was what made him dangerous to her—his ability to bring her to the brink of climax with his voice.

"No," she choked and rolled away, aware of the thin satin that was riding up her thighs. It would take nothing for him to brush that out of his way and give her the orgasm she craved however he chose to deliver it.

Behind her, he made a noise that was both resigned and amused. "Another time, then. Good night, Claudine."

She lay awake a long time, thinking, *When?*

Felipe's mother was aghast. That was what struck Claudine like a slap as she performed her curtsy to the King and Queen.

Queen Paloma radiated appalled astonishment, clearly blindsided by this impromptu invasion of her morning by her firstborn and the substandard fiancée he'd brought with him. She didn't speak for a full minute, only kept her pink-painted lips in a tight purse. Her stunned yellow-brown eyes pierced like a stiletto into Claudine's lungs as Claudine politely murmured that it was an honor to meet them.

The Queen's voice was thin as parchment paper as she asked something in Italian.

"English, please, Mamma. Yes, you're correct. Claudine is the missing contestant."

Claudine turned one of her pageant smiles onto the Queen. She had a well-practiced arsenal that ran a gamut from a resting expression of poise, worn when waiting in the wings but still likely to be caught on camera, to the full-wattage smile held for long minutes when stuck on stage waiting like a mannequin for the rest of the contestants to be introduced and take their place.

In this instance, she found a midrange smile of polite attention, one she would reserve for a conversation with a judge.

This was not a pageant, though. Rather than the armor of a ball gown and full makeup, she wore an understated three-quarter skirt in navy blue with a matching jacket, ensuring her scrapes were all hidden. Her white blouse had a lace tab collar and she'd had Ippolita pull her hair into a demure chignon. Hopefully, her light coat of face powder hid the bruise on her cheek and the worst of her flush as she faced the Queen's blunt, "No" of rejection.

"I've approved the union," King Enzo stated.

"Why? You're not *that* close to death!" the Queen scoffed.

A silence landed so hard in the room Claudine

dropped her wide-eyed gaze to the floor, expecting it to be split wide open. The King was ill? This would be the detail Felipe had not wanted to share with her yesterday.

"Does Francois know?" the Queen asked of Felipe. "Did you take her from his pageant deliberately, to put him in this awkward position? Or has she taken it upon herself to attempt this climb from pageant princess to—? No. Surely you can see that she is the worst sort of opportunist. Enzo?"

"Insults you may speak in Italian," Felipe said coldly. "So my fiancée doesn't have to hear them. But if you must know, Francois sent her to me." Felipe glanced at Claudine, providing her with an opportunity to elaborate if she so chose.

Her throat locked up.

When her reaction was only a subtle recoil at being put on the spot, he smoothly added, "Any embarrassment that Francois suffers around the pageant is very much of his own making. One way or another, this will be the last year his pageant comes to Nazarine."

"Do not try to distract me with that old argument. What do you mean that Francois sent her to you?" his mother demanded.

"Ask him," Felipe invited. "Ah," he said as there was a muted ping from some hidden device. "That will be Vinicio. I had him fetch something from the vault." He opened the door long enough to accept whatever it was.

"You are not giving her any of the crown jewelry," the Queen stated hotly.

"No, Mamma. Just the ring that Great-Aunt Ysabelle bequeathed to me."

"Not—? *No*, Felipe." His mother was truly shaken now, but Felipe seemed to have no pity for his mother.

"This belonged to Queen Giulia," Felipe said to Claudine. "It was given to her daughter, my father's aunt. She never married." Felipe held out his hand in a request for hers. His steady gaze seemed to insist she read every significance into the fact he had chosen to give her this particular ring, because he likened her to that Queen who had been trapped, yet had triumphantly lived by her own rules.

Her hand was shaking as she allowed him to thread the ruby-red stone with its frame of diamonds onto her finger. He brought her cold hand to his mouth and kissed her knuckles.

"I'll have Vinicio release the announcement," Felipe said. "It includes a balcony wave at eleven." He started to draw Claudine from the room.

"No, Felipe." His mother stood, all of her visibly shaking.

Felipe paused, but didn't look at her. He glanced at his father.

King Enzo nodded once.

Felipe's mouth curled into the faintest hint of a smug smile and they left.

While he spoke to Vinicio, Claudine clenched her fist and stared at the blood-red stone on her finger, wondering, *What have I done?*

Felipe did not pander to things like brand and image the way his mother and brother did. He didn't "sell a story" because he didn't have to—even though he knew that eschewing such things was its own brand.

However, he was not blind to the popularity of a good, old-fashioned fairy tale. When a prince chose to marry a commoner, he made anything seem possible. When that commoner was favored to win a contest where half the country had already judged her the most beautiful and deserving, when they were already rooting for her and had grown worried for her because she had disappeared, it became a sensation. The part where she turned up at the side of the Crown Prince, seemingly no worse for wear, created the sort of fervor a public relations specialist could only dream of.

It amused him that his mother was so appalled by Claudine that she had taken the far end of the balcony away from her. She didn't appreciate how well these pageants had prepared Claudine for this. She was not only flawless, having changed into an ivory coatdress and matching hat, she radiated grace and dignity as she offered a gentle wave.

The crowd had begun to amass outside the gates minutes after their announcement. It was now a throng who cheered so loudly the noise seemed to resound in his chest cavity.

"They're waiting for a kiss," he told Claudine. So was he, but he only watched to see how she reacted.

There was the tiniest crack in her composure, one that caused her smile to falter as she turned to face him.

He knew long-lens cameras would be trained on them. He was deliberate in the way he drew her close with one arm around her waist. He held her left hand so the ring would be visible where he cradled it against his chest.

He hadn't been able to stop thinking of her in his bed last night, when the very air had seemed to be soaked with their mutual desire. Or her in the bathtub, when those snowy drifts of bubbles had hidden all but her shiny shoulders and upper chest from his sight. He wanted her naked beneath him so badly that he was in danger of revealing his lust right here in front of the world.

It was probably evident on his face, given the small shiver that went through her and the way her eyes widened before she dampened her lips with her tongue.

"I don't want to ruin your lipstick." He very much wanted to ruin her lipstick, but he kept his kiss as chaste as possible while also lingering long enough to feel the satisfying cling of her lips to his when he lifted his head. Damn, this need for restraint was erotic. He could have groaned out his suffering, it was so sharp.

The crowd cheered even louder while Claudine dropped her lashes, shy and disconcerted.

"Am I wearing your shade?" he asked, still holding her.

"Only a little." She touched the corner of his mouth, causing yet more wild enthusiasm from their audience.

They shared a rueful smile, then her gaze flicked past him and she stiffened. When she would have drawn away, he kept his arm locked around her, waiting for her gaze to come back to his.

"Your mother isn't pleased." Tension crept in around her eyes. "I think this might have been a horrible mistake."

Felipe expected she would feel that way often. "I gave up trying to earn her approval before I was old enough to ask for it."

It was a throwaway comment, one that was

meant to be self-deprecating and to advise her not to take his mother's attitude to heart.

"That makes me sad," she said with earnest sympathy.

He dropped his arm from around her, prickling on the inside. Not angry, but disturbed. He covered it by picking up her hand, offering another orchestrated wave that invited another cheer.

He felt Claudine studying him. "May I ask… What your mother said to your father this morning… Is he—"

"Yes," he confirmed, not allowing his expression to change. It was a fact that his father was terminally ill, not something that caused him to feel anything, one way or another, and that, too, was probably pitiful.

He found himself squeezing her hand. Gently, but doing it all the same. Why? Was he trying to warn her against expressing more sympathy? Or was it driven by something closer to that hollow sensation that seemed to condense around him when he let himself think of his father's impending death?

"That's need-to-know. Please don't discuss it with anyone," he told her, brushing away those pointless emotions.

"I won't," she promised.

Below, the insistent blare of a horn drew their attention. A red cabriolet demanded access as

Francois drove it down the narrow path between the cordoned-off crowd. His arrival raised yet another cacophony of reaction.

When he had cut through the gates and parked below them, he stepped out of his car to send a filthy look upward.

"Do I have to see him?" Claudine's hand tightened on his, her nails digging into his skin hard enough to threaten drawing blood.

"I'll have Vinicio escort you to my room, but I need to speak with him."

"What will you say?" she asked warily.

"That if he ever comes near you again, I will kill him."

"Felipe—" She looked shocked as she searched his eyes. "Are you really that violent?"

He could be. He was starting to realize he was exactly that primal and possessive where she was concerned.

"I speak the only language he understands," he said, drawing her inside and directing Vinicio to take her in one direction while he went the other.

Francois must have taken the grand staircase two at a time, trying to catch them on the balcony. He strode down the main gallery in a rush of rage toward Felipe, looking past him, but Claudine was already gone.

"I tried to call you," Queen Paloma said plaintively, coming inside from the balcony.

Francois ignored her.

"In what universe do you think I will let this happen?" The heat of Francois's breath accosted Felipe's nose.

Felipe kept his feet rooted to the floor, giving up not so much as a millimeter as his brother's fury burned like a conflagration in front of his face.

"What bothers you more?" Felipe asked lazily. "That I've found a bride so quickly? Or that she would rather die than spend another minute with you?"

"Is that what she told you?" Francois backed off a hair, trying to convey his contempt for the both of them.

"She told me exactly what happened," Felipe said with icy loathing. "I'll be sure you're sent a copy of her statement before she releases it."

Francois's eye ticked. His brother was nothing if not versatile, though. He quickly switched tacks.

"She's not revolted by you?" Francois asked with a scathing glance at Felipe's scar. It was meant to remind him that his brother had bested him once.

Once.

Felipe had come to appreciate the scar, despite nearly losing his eye. He had also lost his brother that day, realizing once and for all that Francois would never see him as anything but a rival. By then, Felipe had hated his own reflection, seeing only his brother when he looked in a mirror. He had felt haunted by Francois. Watched.

The scar was a gift. It made it clear that the man he faced in the mirror was himself, not Francois. He had no regrets that he wore it.

"You may come to the wedding if Mamma insists. Otherwise, you will stay away from her. Do *not* test me on this. I promise you the consequences will be deadly."

CHAPTER SEVEN

INITIALLY, THE CONSULTATION in Paris was overwhelming, given it was a much higher octave than what Claudine was used to. She often met with a designer, but usually only for a few minutes. She was occasionally invited to a fashion show and had a good sense of what styles made the most of her attributes. She understood the finer points, too. Some pageants wanted a glamorous look while others wanted something sexier.

Despite all of that, she wasn't prepared for two hours of presentations by world-class designers, each offering a portfolio that outlined their particular strengths and forecasts for future trends.

It struck her that she wasn't shopping for a few outfits. She was curating a wardrobe for a princess. That was a tremendous responsibility. She was relieved when Felipe entered the room.

Everyone stood.

Were they supposed to do that? Claudine rose, too, warming with that infernal suffusion of awareness whenever her fiancé was nearby. He came to buss her cheek with his lips, filling her senses with the sharp aroma of his aftershave.

"How goes the battle?" he asked.

"Everyone is enormously talented." She sent a reassuring smile around the room, wanting to convey that she was pleased with everything she'd seen and hoped to include everyone.

"But?"

A small jolt went through her. She flashed a look up to him. How had he sensed this small conflict in her?

"Everyone has presented a strong theme. Elegant, classic, dignified, sophisticated." She nodded at different sketches. "It's a matter of deciding which is the right direction to lean into."

He scanned the images with a more thoughtful expression.

Claudine waited for him to make a pronouncement for her, but he only said, "There's nothing here to quarrel with. All of them are appropriate for the wife of a future king."

"That's my concern." She tapped her lips. "It looks as though I'm trying too hard to prove I belong. If I doubt it, others will, too. I need to convey all of those things, but there needs to be a broader, overarching theme that…" She searched for a way to convey what seemed to be missing.

"An astute observation." Felipe's gaze on her altered, warming with admiration.

Holding his stare caused her to blush. She shyly lowered her lashes.

"Romanzesco," the Nazarinian designer murmured. *"Amore."*

"Mais bien sûr," another agreed in a tone of discovery.

Now the designers were all looking at each other and nodding. "She is his future queen because they are in love."

"Oh. I—" Claudine nearly strangled on her own tongue.

"Shh. You've given them the key. Let them unlock it," he whispered in her ear, trailing his lips into her neck and sending a shiver chasing down her spine.

There was a curl of cynicism at the corner of his mouth when he lifted his head, though. His caress on her jaw was both tender and ironic. He lightly tilted up her chin and dropped a kiss on her lips before nodding and walking out again.

"This is our only free night," Felipe had told her an hour ago, when she had finished her meetings with the designers. "Once we get to New York, we'll have engagements every night. You'll want to see your mother and you'll be busy with hiring your staff. Let's go out for dinner. Have a date."

Technically, it was her second public appearance as his fiancée, but the pressure to make the right impression was enormous. She chose a silver gray sheath with contoured ruching that had the sex appeal of a feminine silhouette without being outright sexy.

Its three-quarter hem covered her healing scrapes without hiding them completely. The one on her arm was visible through the lace on her sleeve if someone cared to look hard enough. She didn't want to advertise her injuries, but she refused to pretend they hadn't happened.

She arranged her hair in a soft twist with a few loose tendrils and kept her makeup subtle. The bruise on her cheek was all but gone.

"You look beautiful," Felipe said when she nervously presented herself. "If naked."

"Wha—? Oh." A flutter of nervousness had her touching her bare throat as he presented a flat, book-sized velvet case.

She opened the case expecting a necklace, but not one so charming and pretty. The extravagant arrangement of pink and white diamonds made a full circle. The pink stones were all approximately the same size, but cut in different shapes of square, round and pear shapes. Each was framed in glittering white diamonds.

"It's beautiful." She didn't insult him by asking if it was real. "Will you?" She turned.

The necklace descended before her eyes and the

cool weight of it settled against her collarbone. His fingertips tickled at the top of her spine, then his warm mouth touched her nape, nearly taking out her knees. The man was diabolical!

Catching her breath, she moved to the mirror to admire it.

"I've never worn anything so lovely. Who do I say it came from?"

"Me." His drawled tone said, *Obviously*.

"Wait." She spun and touched it. "This isn't a *gift*. It's just for show. Isn't it?" She thought she might faint.

"It's both." There was that tone again, the one that laughed at her for her naivety.

The necklace perfectly reflected the theme of romance and love, yet she felt neither from him as she traced the cool shapes of the stones. She dropped her hand to her side.

"Felipe… I can't accept this."

He sobered as he studied her. "Given all that I expect of you, Claudine, I suggest you become very brazen about what you will accept as compensation. Shall we go?"

She didn't know what to say to that, so she let him guide her toward the door, but the weight of the necklace sat much more heavily upon her.

A private dining room would have been much simpler, security-wise. Felipe would also have preferred to have Claudine to himself, but he had asked Vinicio to arrange for them to dine at an exclusive restaurant that catered to corporate heirs and Europe's nobility. The decor was a waterfall of dripping chandeliers and mirrored finishes, providing suitable sparkle as he showcased their new partnership.

Everyone turned their heads as they were shown to the best table. Felipe was used to that, but tonight they weren't staring at him. They were mesmerized by the radiant woman he escorted.

He had been aware of the challenges she would face as a red-blooded American and not a blue-blooded aristocrat. After Felipe's threats, Francois might think twice about coming for Claudine, but their mother would pick apart every choice she made. Queen Paloma had her own back channels and social circles who would attack Claudine's ability to call herself worthy of a royal marriage.

When Felipe had checked on her wardrobe selection process, he had been looking for armor. He had wanted her to wear those refined styles in the sketches, the ones that would have allowed her to blend in.

She had taken him aback with her insight and he was still laughing with delight at her brilliance. Of course, they must sell a story of love at first sight. Of course. Besotted people were allowed to be impulsive and would be forgiven for any missteps.

Not that Claudine made a single one. She looked flawless as he held her chair then took his seat across from her.

He was the one who thought he might have miscalculated when her sheer beauty dried his throat. He found himself picking up her hand not to maintain an illusion of infatuation, but because he was unable to resist touching her.

Her gaze swept from the glittering city lights beyond the window to his eyes. Questions shimmered in the depths of her dilated pupils.

Inside him, something shifted as though a single brick scraped an inch out of place from an otherwise thick, weathered, impervious wall. He ignored the sensation and stroked his thumb across her knuckles.

Her lashes quivered and she swallowed.

Their server appeared with the first glass of wine from the menu that Vinicio had arranged for them.

When they were alone, she said, "Will you tell me exactly what you're expecting from me?" Her voice faded as he let his brows go up. She pulled her hand from his. "For instance, is your laughing at me something I should learn to tolerate?"

"I can't help that I find it amusing when you speak to me in a way no one else does. Not outside of my family, at least, and I don't like them, so they don't count."

"You don't like any of them?" She seemed distressed by that, even though she'd met all of them. She had to see it was warranted.

"I liked my aunt." He nodded at her ring. "She died when I was still a child."

She searched his expression, giving him time to expound on that, but he didn't intend to. His affection for the outspoken woman had been as close to a grandmotherly relationship as he'd had. She had lived a long, good life, but the loss of her still stung.

After a moment, Claudine pressed her lips and gave a nod of acceptance.

"I guess I'm wondering what I'll do. We've spoken about children, but I've always assumed I would work in some capacity even after I had a family. Both of my mothers did. I can't imagine being idle."

"What were you planning to do after the pageant?"

"I don't know," she sighed. "I've never known, to be honest. I think that's why I kept entering them, so I wouldn't have to make that decision. I do well enough in science and sports and art, but I'm not particularly gifted with any of them. I enjoy learning new things, but I lose interest very quickly. My looks have always felt like my one asset that was extraordinary. That will fade with age, so I'm exploiting it while I can," she said ruefully.

"You think your looks will fade? I highly doubt it. Nor do I think that's why you win pageants."

"They're *beauty* contests," she pointed out.

"They're contests. And you're competitive as hell."

"No, I'm not." Her brows came together, perplexed.

"You don't see it?"

"No."

He made a noncommittal noise, not interested in arguing the point, but all he could see in his mind's eye was her, kneeling on the beach, proving her superiority to his brother without even needing a witness to it. She hadn't been broken when Felipe had approached her. She had thrown sand in his face and continued to fight.

Damn. Now he was back to wanting to touch her.

"Let's dance." He rose and held out his hand.

Claudine didn't remember what they ate, only the way it felt to be in his arms.

If this was the seduction Felipe had promised her, it was subtle. It wasn't what he did, but what he didn't do that bombarded her with yearning.

His fingertips brushed the bare skin on her

shoulder, but only in passing, not lingering. The shape of his mouth in her sightline filled her with curiosity to feel his lips against hers, but he denied her. The press of his hand at her hip was hot and possessive and stayed exactly where it was, no matter how she willed him to cup her breast or fondle her backside.

When the heat of his breath stirred her hair against her ear, and he asked, "Shall we skip dessert?" she was weak with longing for more. Her skin felt electric, her blood molten.

"Yes," she said, feeling drugged.

Paparazzi had gathered outside, blinding them with their flashes as they slid into the Rolls-Royce. They were no sooner inside than they were stuck in traffic.

"An event has just let out, Your Highness. I apologize for the delay," the driver said.

"Do your best." Felipe said and pressed the button to close the privacy screen. "I don't want to wait until the hotel to kiss you. *Come here.*"

The rough command in his voice undid her. The windows were so dark it was nearly impossible to see the lights of the city through them, so she slipped from her seat, which was as deep and luxurious as a recliner, past the wide console between them and into his lap.

With a gruff noise, he gathered her close, enclosing her in the warm cage of his embrace. His mouth settled across hers in a searing brand of heat. His tongue slid past the seam of her lips, the blatant act sending a spear of pure lust straight into the pit of her belly.

While his hands roamed all over her back and breast and hip and thigh, exactly as she had been aching for him to do, she burrowed beneath the edges of his jacket, wanting the man beneath the layers of wool and silk tie and the shirt made of a fabric with such a high thread count it felt as though he was naked beneath luxury sheets.

When she felt the release of her gown's zipper, she drew back slightly.

"No?" He stalled his touch.

She looked to the tinted the windows, but it was so dark back here onlookers probably couldn't even tell she was in his lap.

"No, it's okay."

His mouth came back to hers and the zipper went down to her lower back. She pulled her arm free of one sleeve.

"No bra. I thought not." His head swooped and her nipple was drawn into such a cavern of heat and pull she gasped at the sharp sensation. The damp scorch sent sweet runnels of urgent desire racing to collect in her loins.

"Felipe," she sobbed, wriggling, so acutely aroused she didn't know how to process it.

"Did I not promise to give you pleasure, *cara*

mia?" His voice was far from his usual cultured tone and made everything in her twist with need. "Let's put your foot here in the cup holder."

He guided her shoe heel to the console so she had one knee raised against his chest, the other dangling off his thigh. In a small shift, she was cradled deeper in his lap so the thick shape of his arousal pressed to the cheek of her bottom.

As his touch drew patterns along the inside of her thigh, climbing beneath her skirt, she shook. The ache in her core intensified.

"Say you want this," he commanded softly.

"I do. *Yes*."

His features were shadowed and dark, the line of his mouth a cruel tilt. But his tracing touch was barely there as he explored the lace of her underwear.

"Give me your mouth. I want to kiss you again."

She tightened her arms around his neck, sealing her lips to his while his devilish touch continued to draw those maddening lines down her center, the pressure too light. Too teasing.

In a flagrant move, she thrust her tongue into his mouth, trying to tell him how badly she needed *more*.

In an equally deliberate move, he picked up the gusset of her undies and shifted it to the side, baring her damp flesh to the cool air of the back seat.

She looked again at the driver and the guard,

both silhouettes facing forward through the dark privacy window, both oblivious to what the Crown Prince was doing to her.

He tipped her another degree off balance and ducked to steal another taste of her nipple. At the same time, he began to explore the wet seam of her sex, parting her folds, deepening his caress, exploring and invading. Claiming.

She released a guttural moan of unrestrained joy, clenching on his finger as he made love to her with his hand. He suckled at her breast and danced her toward an elusive pinnacle.

"Hurry, *cara mia*," he lifted his head to coax. "We're almost there." His touch rolled and pressed, growing insistent. "And so are you."

With another sob of abandonment, she caught his hand and held his touch where she needed it. She crushed her mouth to his and ground her hips and *broke*, flying outward in a thousand pieces. It was so powerful she turned her face into his neck, every breath a cry of ecstasy while he continued to caress her and murmur in Italian, holding her tight with his other arm, keeping her safe while she shook.

Slowly she came back to herself, still trembling and weak. She was dimly aware of him fixing her underwear and lowering her leg and helping her thread her arm back into the sleeve of her dress before he drew her zipper up.

"That is another compensation I want you to be brazen about accepting." His lips pressed to hers with something like tenderness. "I enjoyed that very much."

"Do you…" She was still befuddled, but she was aware of the prod of his arousal against her hip. "Should I…?"

"I'll wait. Go back to your seat. The car has stopped and I can see paparazzi is already gathered here, too."

Felipe didn't want to wait. His body didn't. Pleasuring Claudine and feeling the intensity of her response had nearly put him over the edge behind the sealed fly of his trousers. He longed to lose himself in her for hours. Days.

But therein lay the issue. He would lose himself in the process. He had known this lust between them was powerful. Now he knew exactly how all-consuming it could become, and that simply would not do.

As they entered their royal suite overlooking avenue Montaigne and the Eiffel Tower, Claudine's maid appeared in the door to the bedroom they were sharing.

Felipe had interviewed Ippolita himself before giving her the opportunity to prove herself to Claudine. She had been suitably intimidated by him and very earnest in her admiration for his fiancée. She didn't speak English and he had encouraged her to keep it that way, to help Claudine learn Italian, but also because it was useful in situations like this when he wanted to speak to Claudine without her maid following every word.

"You head to bed," Felipe said to Claudine. "I have calls to make."

"I thought—" Claudine's cheekbones scorched red. Her confused gaze searched his.

"Run a bath," he told Ippolita in Italian, who nodded and hurried away.

"I don't understand." Claudine's brow pleated with hurt. Tension came in around her mouth. There was accusation there, too, and defensiveness in the way she folded her arms so tightly across the breasts he had worshipped. "Did I do something wrong in the car?"

"Not at all. I enjoyed our interlude as much as you did. This is not a rejection, Claudine." It was an exercise in self-discipline.

"What then? A power trip?" Her troubled expression hardened into a glare, one sheened by angry tears. "I thought we were sharing something. Ourselves, maybe, but you were actually proving how helpless you can make me feel?"

She had been delightfully at his mercy, yet sensuously demanding in the way she had pressed his hand to her mound and moaned into his mouth. It had been exquisite.

"I wanted to give you pleasure." He had reveled in it. "It's as simple as that. You asked what you should expect from our marriage and I showed you."

"Yes, I'm beginning to fully grasp what I should expect—to be treated like a toy." A strident note had entered her voice. It annoyed him.

"I do not view you as a toy." He was well aware she was a fully grown, hot-blooded woman. "I'm merely avoiding any slip-ups that could result in a pregnancy that is not seen as wholly legitimate." That wasn't entirely a prevarication.

Behind her shock, a shadow of profound injury moved across her expression.

"You're still worried that I might be carrying Francois's—"

"No," he said firmly. "But a pregnancy test is probably a good idea. The pageants might discourage you from having relationships, but that doesn't mean there haven't been any men in your recent past, does it?"

"I've actually never had a man in my 'past,'" she snapped, putting air quotes around the word. "Recently or otherwise."

For a moment, he was uncharacteristically speechless.

"Am I understanding you correctly?" he asked with genuine astonishment. "Are you saying you've never had intercourse? How old are you?"

"Twenty-three." She glared at him with resentment at his questioning her, but it was so incredibly unusual in this day and age, he genuinely couldn't grasp it.

"But you're a very passionate person. Have you had lovers who *aren't* men?"

"Oh my God! This is why women can't win. If we have sex, we're sluts. If we don't, we're liars. Thanks for a *lovely* evening." She slammed the bedroom door behind her.

That wasn't what he'd been saying at all. He was tempted to go after her and tell her that, but he'd got what he wanted, hadn't he? Sex was definitely off the table.

Before her bath, Claudine used the translation app on her phone to ask Ippolita to get her a pregnancy test.

She left the negative result on the back of the toilet for Felipe to find when he rose the next morning, still furious with him.

Maybe if she had actually thrown it in his face there would have been some satisfaction in it, but as it was, she only felt falsely accused. Used. She had felt helpless to his caresses last night, which had been okay when she had thought he had merely stopped because the car had, but the way he had touched her so intimately, then seemed completely unaffected by the experience kept striking as a hot iron of shame deep in her belly. She was already in an unequal position with him. That had only driven his superiority home in the worst possible way.

"That wasn't necessary," he said blithely about the test when he joined her for breakfast. "I believed you."

She snorted, not believing *that*.

His phone dinged and he glanced at it. "Vinicio would like to go over some résumés with you, but that can wait until we're in the air."

Her heart lurched. "I like Ippolita." Had she got her maid into trouble, asking for that test?

"You'll need a full staff of your own since a number of royal duties and foundations will fall under your purview. You won't be idle."

"Oh." She pondered that. She liked the idea of learning about different charities and initiatives, playing ambassador for a good cause, but after last night, she was teetering in and out of thinking she had made a horrible mistake by agreeing to marry him.

On the one hand, she shimmered in echoes of the profound pleasure that had gripped her as she had clung to him, convulsing in his lap. It had been everything he had promised and more, but she couldn't recollect her pleasure without the fires of embarrassment also trying to engulf her. The way he had so easily rebuffed her afterward kept slapping her in the face, forcing her to realize how enormous the power imbalance was between them.

Maybe when they got to New York, she would just break things off and stay there.

The scrape of her spoon into her bowl of yogurt suddenly seemed very loud.

She glanced up to find Felipe watching her shrewdly. Her heart lurched with the sense that he had read her thoughts.

"You're still upset with me," he said.

"Of course not," she lied coolly. "Why would I be?" She rose. "I have to finalize with the designers before we go. Excuse me."

He caught her hand as she tried to brush past him.

She paused to look down on him, not pulling away because—damn her soul—she liked the feel of his thumb sliding over the inside of her wrist, even though he could probably feel her pulse tripping.

"You can't walk away every time a conversation becomes uncomfortable. We'll never speak," he said dryly. "I thought you were being overly sensitive last night, but I've since realized your inexperience made our lovemaking take on more meaning for you."

"I'm not being overly sensitive." How humiliating. She tried to pull away, but he held on, not rough about it, simply conveying an urge for her to continue listening.

"You're upset because you allowed me more liberties than you've ever allowed any man and I didn't seem to appreciate that. I do now."

She twisted free of his grip.

"I'm upset because I felt manipulated. Go ahead and deny it, but I won't believe you," she threw at him. "I'm pretty, not stupid. You keep talking about how we need to trust each other, but how can we if we're not going to be honest with each other?" A thread of despair entered her tone as she saw endless suspicions and avoided truths unspooling into the future. It wouldn't work. It couldn't. "You wanted to control me and you did. Why the hell would I want to marry that?"

She felt his stare like the concentrated heat of sunlight through a magnifying glass, trying to penetrate her skin.

When she met his gaze, his eye ticked, betraying his inner tension.

"It's not you I was trying to control." He rose so abruptly she gasped and fell back a step. "It was myself. I want you, Claudine. More than is healthy."

His hands descended on her, fingertips gripping her shoulders through the plush velvet of her robe. She threw her arms up between them, but he didn't try to pull her any closer, only held her before him.

"You want honesty? Then stand here and listen to it. The way you fell apart in the car is all I can think about. I want to tear open your robe and clear that table and eat you for breakfast. I want us to break every piece of furniture in here and, after that taste last night, I'm confident we will. When the time is right." He searched her expression with lust in his eyes and concern pulling his brow. "After what you told me—that you're a virgin—I have even more reason to stay this side of rational, otherwise I might unwittingly hurt you."

She couldn't seem to catch a full breath. His strong hands on her upper arms were probably the only thing holding her up.

"The fact that you responded that strongly to my touch, Claudine…" He slid his hands upward to cup her jaw. His thumbs rested at the corners of her mouth. "We're a dangerous combination. Do you understand that?"

He might be right. She had the most indecent urge to turn her head and open her mouth so she could suck on his thumb.

His fingers splayed and he slowly trailed his touch down her throat where he spread the edges of the robe to expose more of her collarbone.

"Are your nipples hard? Shall I feel for myself?"

"Yes," she breathed, eyes fluttering closed.

Her arms fell away as his light touch stole beneath the lapels of the robe, loosening the belt as his hands found her naked breasts and caressed the swells, fingertips grazing the turgid points of her nipples. They stood tall and eager against his light pinch. Dampness gathered between her thighs.

"I bet you could come just from this, if we had time," he murmured, lowering his head so his breath washed across lips that stung as hard as her nipples. "Touch yourself. Let me watch."

It was such a flagrant request she dragged her eyes open, fearful he was taunting her for his own amusement.

If he had been, she didn't know what she would have done because she was willing to do nearly anything he asked, he had that much of a hold over her. It was a disturbing realization. It would have been outright terrifying if there hadn't been a glaze of blind lust in his eyes that mirrored what was going on inside herself. Nothing more sinister, just pure animalistic craving.

Recognizing that sent a drive of compulsion through her, one that wanted to see how far she could push him past his discipline. How far could they push each other?

That was sobering. She checked herself from

throwing herself into his arms. He was right. They were a potent combination.

"Now you see." He gently withdrew his touch from inside the robe and doubled it closed again, as though bundling her against an arctic wind.

Then he gathered her close in a hug that would have been purely one of consolation if she hadn't felt the press of his arousal through the layers of robe and trousers.

"Make no mistake about how much I want you, Claudine. I want you more than I've ever wanted anyone in my life. But once we start that fire, it may incinerate us both."

CHAPTER EIGHT

"MOM." CLAUDINE DIDN'T realize how much stress she'd been under until she almost burst into tears at the sight of her mother.

She wanted to crash into her, but she had learned as a child to open her arms and wait for her mother to hug her first so Claudine could take her cue from the strength and length of her mother's hug as to how hard and long she could hug her back. Today, she was wrapped up in a good, strong one that let her soak up some of the reassurance she desperately needed.

She could have stayed there all day, but Ann-Marie drew back. "Introduce me to your fiancé."

Claudine did and watched Felipe gently take the hand her mother offered and simply cover it with his own, being so careful with her it squeezed Claudine's heart to see it.

"How are you feeling?" he asked her. "Are they treating you well here?"

"Better than the celebrities. I feel like a quee—Um…" She sent a perplexed look to Claudine.

"Good." Felipe's mouth twitched and he released her.

"It's okay, Mom." Her mother was down-to-earth and not impressed by fame or wealth, always far more interested in character or heart. "We wanted you here for privacy as much as medical care, but how are your symptoms? Are they settling down at all?"

They caught up on her mother's condition. Thanks to the clinic's doting doctors, her pain had already receded to manageable levels. She was eating and sleeping well, which always helped calm her symptoms, but she was still suffering vision loss and had begun using a walker as a precaution against stumbling. Aside from worrying about her daughter, her mental health was positive, though.

"It's very expensive," Ann-Marie whispered to Claudine when Felipe excused himself to take a call. "How are you paying for this? Are you really marrying him? Or is this a publicity stunt for the pageant? Have you read what they say about him? And what they're saying about you?"

"I know, Mom. Try to ignore all that. And yes, it's real. I know it's rushed, but…" Her mother would never accept that her daughter was marrying for her benefit. Or that Claudine was allowing herself to be used as a pawn, no matter how terrible Francois was or that a kingdom hung in the balance. "But this is something I feel is the right thing to do."

A better word might have been *inevitable*. She was still shaken by the things Felipe had said in Paris. They hadn't so much as held hands since. They'd been tied up with staff and travel and other things, but there was a force field of electricity that seemed to contain them inside a shared bubble, making her prickle with discomfort while he was out of the room, then softening to a delicious tingle when he returned.

"Forgive me, Ann-Marie. I have a punishing schedule while we're here, but I wanted Claudine to have this time with you to reassure you both." His energy rushed in to swirl like autumn leaves around the room. When he took the empty armchair, he didn't so much settle as coil with readiness in it. "Has she explained that I'd like to hire you a private nurse, to help stave off these flareups and manage them when they happen? There are also clinics in Europe that are closer to us in Nazarine, which you might prefer so Claudine can see you more readily. She tells me that rest helps, so I was thinking that, after the wedding, I could make my yacht available to you. Or you could visit any of my residences if you'd like to stay on dry land. Perhaps invite a friend and simply enjoy quiet time to recuperate?"

"Oh my goodness. That's not necessary. I like my life here in New York," her mother said with a polite but firm smile.

"Then I'll arrange security to ensure you're not bothered too badly, but please let me do these things, Ann-Marie. Claudine's agreement to marry me has implications for you that I want to mitigate as much as possible. The paparazzi can be a nuisance, as I'm sure your neighbors are already aware."

"I—" She looked again to Claudine. "When exactly is the wedding?"

"We haven't set—"

"June twenty-second," Felipe said.

"What?" Claudine snapped her head around. It was already the fourth. "When did you decide that?"

"My father's team has just confirmed the twenty-second will work."

Claudine was speechless while her mother's wide-eyed stare asked her if she had parted ways with every single one of her marbles.

"Time is a finite resource in my world, I'm afraid." Felipe rose. "I know you both have a lot to talk about and plan, but Claudine and I have a number of engagements this week. We're already running late. I'll have a car take you back to your home tonight, though. You can meet with Claudine tomorrow to discuss all your options and make a plan for your travel to Nazarine for the wedding."

There was nothing heartening in seeing her mother blink the way Claudine did, breathless at the pace Felipe set. Claudine could feel her mother's concern as they hugged goodbye. She promised a proper chat tomorrow, but her stomach churned with misgivings as she reboarded the helicopter that had brought them from the private airfield after they'd landed in the royal jet.

The helicopter's cabin was small, holding only four luxurious leather armchairs. *Only* four. The other two were occupied by Vinicio and a guard, both of whom offered to serve them from the selection of beverages, chocolate, and nuts that were within Claudine's reach.

She wanted to speak privately to Felipe, but had to wait until they had landed on the rooftop helipad of what seemed to be a residential skyscraper. Staff awaited them as they came out of the elevator into an ultramodern penthouse suite where huge windows showcased the fading sunset.

"Welcome back, Your Highness."

Felipe introduced Claudine to everyone, then Ippolita whisked her away to an opulent bedroom where a stylist had a selection of gowns for Claudine to choose from.

It was her first formal evening with Felipe, a black-tie welcome dinner ahead of an international trade forum that Felipe would attend tomorrow. Then they had a gala on Friday night and an opera on Saturday.

Claudine nervously selected a dramatic, off-the-shoulder gown in midnight blue with a straight cut and a slit that would flash its silver lining when she walked.

The scrape on her shin would be visible, as would the one on her arm, but they were healing quickly, thanks to an ointment that Ippolita had provided. With a bit of spray tan applied atop them, they were fairly inconspicuous.

She removed the gown for some final alterations and had a quick shower to freshen up after their travel, keeping her hair dry.

She slipped on the silk kimono that Ippolita offered, but was too restless to sit for hair and makeup just yet. June twenty-second? *Really?*

Tightening the belt on her kimono, she left her room and went through the lounge, across to the other closed door.

Vinicio glanced up from his tablet with surprise, but nodded when she pointed at the door, silently asking if Felipe was in there.

She knocked and heard, *"Entrare."*

Felipe's room was a mirror of hers, with a huge bed footed by a comfortable bench, a sitting area in the corner, a walk-through closet to a sumptuous bathroom and French doors to a balcony.

He stood near a side table wearing only a towel and a sheen of dampness on his swarthy skin. His musculature was sheer perfection, accentuated by the pattern of hair across his chest and down his sculpted abs. He held a drink half raised to his lips, seemingly arrested by the fact she wasn't Vinicio.

"Um…" She was disconcerted to find him nearly naked. She pressed the door shut to protect his privacy.

"You should leave," he said hoarsely.

His voice made her skin tighten. The air seemed to crackle with static.

"I…" Her throat was very dry, her own voice husked. "I want to talk to you."

"We'll talk in the car."

"I just want to know why we have to get married so fast."

He let out a choked breath and threw back his shot of alcohol.

"I just spent fifteen minutes in the shower thinking of all the things I want to do with you, trying to tame this lust. I mean this with the utmost respect, Claudine, but get the hell out before I start doing them."

She reflexively backed herself into the door, but couldn't help asking, "What kinds of things?"

"Do you completely lack any sense of self-pres-
ervation?" He set aside his glass and stalked toward her. "The kinds of things where you have to
set the limits because I don't have any." He guided
her hand to the door latch near her hip.

It was the only way he touched her and she felt
bereft when his hand fell away from hers. The heat
of his body was a spell that wafted out to para-
lyze her, melting her bones and her ability to think
and any sense of resistance. He smelled fresh and
spicy and intoxicating. She was mesmerized by
the twitch of his nostrils and the tension around
his mouth and the way his scar stood out against
the flush of color that sat under his skin.

"Are we doing this, then?" He hooked one finger into her belt. The slippery silk disintegrated
and the edges fell open.

She didn't move to cover herself, wanting to
see his reaction.

His hot gaze scorched her skin as he slid his
hands inside the robe. He skimmed her shoulders so the loose robe dropped off her shoulders,
leaving her naked. Her breasts were already full
and heavy, aching for his touch as he traced his
fingertips down her arms before he gathered the
swells and gently crushed them.

His mouth came down on hers with equal, tender force.

She moaned at the powerful jolt of need that

rang through her. She had been waiting for this, *yearning* for it, but the maelstrom of sensations was so alarming she sought to catch at anything solid. Her hands found the smooth heat of his biceps, his shoulders, the muscles at the base of his neck and the dampness of his hair.

Then he was gone. She opened her eyes to see him sinking to his knees before her.

"This is what I'm going to do," he warned as his heavy hands clasped the tops of her thighs. His thumbs traced the crease on either side of her naked mound. He waited a pulse beat, allowing her to refuse, then he said with foreboding, *"First."*

He was shockingly blatant, sliding his thumbs to part her and leaning in to paint his tongue across her sensitive flesh in a very flagrant claiming.

She gasped at the intensity of it, but she had nowhere to retreat to. She was pressed to the door and had to swallow her cry of pleasure so Vinicio wouldn't hear it.

Felipe showed her no mercy. His clever mouth and touch swept and invaded and caressed until her entire world shrank to this, only this, the place he pleasured so mercilessly. Within moments she was cresting a pinnacle, suffused in a shower of stars.

As she shook and bit back her cries and tried to find something solid to hold onto, she found only the panels in the door and the fine strands of his hair as he stayed on his knees before her.

"You needed this, didn't you?" He rubbed his lips against her skin. "I know, *cara mia*. Me, too." He sounded both sympathetic and amused.

Then he did it *again*.

Her second orgasm was even more powerful.

She was fully sagged against the door in its aftermath, needing the press of his hot chest to hold her up when he rose to kiss her, long and just a little rough. He still wore his towel. Its fluffy texture pressed the tops of her thighs and cushioned the shape of his erection against her as he used his weight to press her to the wood.

She mindlessly ran her hands over the smooth skin of his shoulders and upper arms, trying to sate an appetite that seemed to have only sharpened, rather than been satisfied.

"Now," he said in a guttural voice, nose brushing hers. "I want you to leave before this goes any further."

Now she found her resistance because *no*. She refused to be the only one who was leveled by this acute hunger while he smugly enjoyed how thoroughly he'd taken her apart.

She touched his shoulder so he took a half step back, then caught the towel to keep him from moving any further than that.

A flare of pure, wild hunger flexed across his expression.

It was all the encouragement she needed to tug open the towel and drop to her knees before him.

Oh. She had never had such a close-up look at a fully aroused man. For a moment, she was all curiosity and shyness and fearful of hurting him, touching him very tentatively.

The way his breath hissed in drew her gaze upward.

"Are you trying to kill me?" His abdomen was sucked hollow, his lips thin with strain.

A delightful wave of power rose within her. She clasped him in her fist and did what he had done to her. She offered a thorough, brazen lick that had him slapping his two hands to the door above her, leaning a fraction closer into the heat of her mouth.

Oh, it was satisfying to feel him shake with desire as she learned his shape and textures and taste. His thigh under her exploring hand was rock-hard, his buttock tense—all of him drawn tight with excitement.

He wasn't nearly so uncontrolled as she had been, though. He pulsed his hips a few times and released noises of barely contained restraint, but after a few moments, he caressed her cheek and said, "You can finish me like this if you want to. It's the most erotic thing I've ever seen or felt, but I want to be inside you, *cara mia*. Would you like that?"

She released him and he helped her rise. He didn't take her to the bed, though. He pressed his body against hers again, trapping her against the cool door again. His hard flesh left its impression against her belly while his hands stole all over her, lighting fresh fires within her as he kissed her again and again.

Her restless hands skated over his taut skin, learning the landscape of his ribs and lower back, his buttocks and flat hips and the pebbled nipples on his chest.

His kiss went into her neck and across her collarbone while his fingers returned to the flesh he had claimed so thoroughly, inciting her all over again, plying and teasing, preparing her to receive a deeper, thicker penetration.

When her inner muscles were clinging to his touch and her hips lifting in invitation, he nuzzled her temple and whispered, "If you want me there, guide me."

"Here?" Against the door?

"It will slow me down." His mouth twisted with self-deprecation. "I won't go too deep or thrust too hard. If you'd rather stop—"

Never.

She felt shameless and overt as she clasped his pulsing flesh and stood on her tiptoes to rub his tip against her slippery, yearning flesh. He bent his knees and here his superior experience came to the fore. Very suddenly, very undeniably, he was penetrating her.

His hand cradled the side of her face. "Look at me. Tell me if it hurts."

"It doesn't. It— *Oh.* A little." The implacable stretch threatened pain, making her bite her lip in apprehension, but she slid her hand to his lower back in a signal for him to continue.

He held still, very still. His eyes glittered behind the screen of his spiky lashes.

"This is the most exquisite hell," he told her with a caress of his thumb against her cheek.

"Please don't stop. I want—" She tilted her hips and brought one knee up to wrap her heel behind his thigh, accepting any pain that might happen because she sensed the pleasure behind it. The fulfillment.

As she pulled him in, there was a fresh sting. Heat. A throb deep inside her and the pressure of his pubic bone against the swollen knot of nerves that sent a gratifying swirl of joy through her pelvis.

With a shaken sigh, he sealed his mouth to hers and dropped his hand from her cheek to cradle her bottom. He used his forearm to hug her leg against his hip. In small, abbreviated thrusts, he ground himself against her, the friction subtle but deliciously effective.

There was something deeply provocative in being trapped this way against an unlocked door, forced to be quiet while such incredible sensuality built inside her. She closed her fist in his hair and sucked on his tongue and reveled in the growing pressure that felt too hot and intense to contain.

Suddenly, he lifted his head and pulled his hips back, only to return in a thrust of couched strength. The flood of pleasure against her sensitized nerve endings was astronomical. She let out a helpless cry, then another as he did it again.

"Now, *cara mia*. Let go. *Now*."

His hips returned to hers. Harder. Faster. He forced all the coiled density of need inside her to collapse and explode. In a rush of exquisite pleasure, she was launched. Flying. Moaning and clinging and arching for more, utterly abandoned in her greed for *all of him*.

He picked her up with both hands beneath her backside and pumped strongly, prolonging her climax so it struck again and again before his whole body crushed her to the door. He strained and shuddered and tipped back his head to release a roar of triumph.

"I'm so embarrassed," Claudine said.

"Why?" Felipe snapped from his doze. Somehow, he had carried her to the bed and scraped back the covers before they'd fallen to the mattress. His attempt to catch his breath had turned into the twilight between reality and dreams.

Actually, that was where he'd been from the moment she had walked through the door.

Virgin, he recalled, and dragged himself into full awareness. He came up on an elbow. He didn't care if she was bleeding on the sheet, but she would feel self-conscious about it.

"Because Vinicio is right outside that door," she whispered with horror, looking toward it. "I didn't even lock it."

"Vinicio would not be my personal secretary if he didn't have the sense to clear the area for a five-kilometer radius when my future wife visits my bedroom wearing nothing more than moisturizer." He fell onto his back again, letting his eyes drift shut, returning to the zen of post-orgasmic high.

"And a robe," she corrected lightly and slithered closer. Her hand came to rest on his chest. "This wasn't why I came in here, you know."

"No? I will maintain an open-door policy in future anyway, hoping for exactly this sort of surprise." He picked up her hand, idly kissing each of her fingertips.

Damn, that had been good. Better than he had imagined it would be, but he didn't let himself devolve into recollections of her taste or her tongue dancing against his sex or the way her powerful orgasm had seemed to prolong his own. He was already too obsessed with her, thinking about sex when he ought to be—

Hell, he was the keynote speaker at tonight's dinner.

He didn't bother glancing at the clock. Vinicio would have sent a message that he was delayed.

"I wanted to ask you why the wedding is happening so quickly. I thought I would have more time to get used to the idea."

"My father doesn't have much time left. He wants to know the throne is secure."

She picked up her head. "Is that why you did this? Had sex with me?" she asked with a note of suspicion in her voice.

"I didn't drag you in here, Claudine. I told you to leave, remember?"

She held his hard stare, searching for ulterior motives.

A sensation struck inside his chest, one as sharp as the blade that had scored his face. It *hurt* that she didn't trust him. And it was all the more intolerable because it was so unexpected. Since when could she reach so far inside him? Was it the consequence of being inside *her*?

"If you don't trust me, why did you let this happen?" he asked with quiet chill.

"I couldn't help it," she admitted in a small

voice. "I needed to know how it would be. How you would feel. How we would make each other feel."

The piercing icicle in his chest melted away.

His hand found its way to her jaw. He cradled her soft cheek, memorizing the way she still wore a heavy-lidded look of sensuality. Her hair was tumbled and her mouth pouted in a way that made him want to—

This was the danger she posed to him!

"We need to dress. We're late for our engagement."

Her brow flinched and her gaze was bruised as she drew her chin out of his palm.

"Such is the life of a royal, my dear. Duty always calls."

He rolled up onto his elbow to press a kiss on her lips, one that he meant to be brisk, but settled and softened into a tender, lingering thing that he hadn't known he was capable of delivering. It hurt, too, deep in his chest, in a way that wasn't as painful. More of a pull, like stretching a stiff muscle.

When he drew back, he was able to breathe easier and words slipped from his lips that he had no idea he was going to say.

"When we return later, I'll be all yours."

CHAPTER NINE

CLAUDINE HAD TOLD her stylist she was unafraid of heights, so her shoes were five-inch silver heels with a bow on the toes. She wore her hair gathered in a sleek topknot and encouraged her stylist to add some drama to her makeup, ensuring her look was well-defined and sophisticated.

When she asked Ippolita for her pink-and-white necklace, Ippolita said something about the Prince having it. Claudine's Italian was progressing at a rapid pace, but she still only caught every third or fourth word.

A bizarre shyness overcame her. She had developed a near unbreakable poise for almost any circumstance when sexuality was abruptly thrust at her—ha ha. But none of those situations had prepared her for a situation where she had actually engaged in sex.

Or for the sense that she now shared something with someone that was bigger than a secret. It was an experience. A profound one.

Did he feel the same? Even a little?

That was the thing she didn't want to face—his potential indifference to something that had left her feeling altered. It wasn't the "I am a woman now" nonsense. It was more the sense that she had shared too much of herself and didn't know how to take it back.

When she was dressed and as flawless as she could possibly feel, she braced herself to walk out to the lounge where she would have to look Felipe in the eye. All sorts of guilty longing were probably flashing neon bright in her face as she entered.

He had put on his tuxedo. Lord, why did he have to be so good-looking? And confident. He wore the addition of his royal sash of green satin with as much casual ease as he wore the shoes that were polished to a mirror finish.

When she appeared, he turned his head and his gaze swept to her toes and came back. Knowledge—so much carnal knowledge—sat as a banked heat behind his narrowed gaze. She was acutely aware they had both run their mouths all over each other's bodies. She had had three orgasms and was tender between her thighs.

There was no mockery in his gaze, though. Only approval. The glow of appreciation in his eyes drew her the way a fire would have beckoned her closer on a cold winter night.

"I, um—" She had to clear a huskiness from her throat. "I asked Ippolita for my necklace. She said you have it?"

Her throat was already dry and grew positively arid when he offered a case covered in silver velvet.

"Not that you need adornment," he said. "You're beautiful without anything at all, as I'm more than aware."

Really? He was going to say something like that in front of Vinicio?

She blushed and flicked a look to his secretary, but Vinicio was doing an excellent impression of a lamppost.

Felipe opened the case to reveal a stunning blue sapphire suspended from a platinum chain. A pair of matching drop earrings nestled beside it.

"I saw these when I bought the other one. I couldn't decide, so I got both."

She was too overwhelmed to speak and wound up standing mutely as he fastened the heavy links around her throat. Her hands shook as she removed her earrings and replaced them with the sapphires.

When she turned back to him, her shoes put her virtually eye to eye with him. A faint smile touched his mouth.

"I like this height." He caressed her jaw and kissed near the corner of her mouth.

"Felipe," she breathed in protest. "I don't want to be bribed."

"We talked about why I like to see you in things that I give you." His fingertip traced the rim of her ear then nudged her earring into swinging.

Why does any man want to put a ring on a woman? To claim her, of course.

Oh, help. He had claimed her. Utterly and thoroughly. She closed her eyes, body paralyzed by the way his fingertips stole into the hollow beneath her ear and caressed her nape, lifting goose bumps on her skin.

"You don't have to leave, Vinicio," Felipe murmured. "We're ready to go."

Oh, Gawd. Felipe's hand fell to catch her own while Claudine tried to pull herself together before she turned to face Vinicio. He smoothly held the door for them, avoiding direct eye contact. They all traveled down the elevator and into a car. Vinicio came in the back with them this time so there was no danger, or opportunity, for backseat seductions.

The rest of the evening was not unlike Claudine's life as a pageant contestant. She smiled and held her best posture without fidgeting. She shook hands and expressed interest in the people she met and stayed on message when people asked about her engagement to Felipe.

"He whisked me off my feet. It's been a whirl-wind."

"And the pageant?" someone asked. "Why did you drop out?"

"I couldn't continue to compete. It would have been a conflict of interest. I miss my friends, obviously, but it's fun to be an observer for once. I can't wait to see who wins." She turned that into asking who that person's favorite was and offered mild inside gossip about this woman's talent or that one's well-publicized struggle to overcome personal adversity.

"And your injuries?" a man asked behind her. "How did those happen?"

Claudine glanced over her shoulder to see a man roughly Felipe's age. He sent Claudine a sly look before turning a more malevolent one onto Felipe.

The blatant implication was that Felipe had inflicted them on her. It was appalling enough to turn Claudine's stomach. She felt Felipe's hand come to the small of her back. His arm was tense, ready to pull her protectively close.

"They happened before I left the pageant," Claudine said, holding the man's gaze without flinching.

"Oh? Is that why you left? You knew you couldn't win all scuffed up like that? Or did you simply find a bigger fish to fry?"

"Have Benedetto removed," Felipe said to Vinicio without otherwise acknowledging the man.

"Your brother is engaged. Have you heard that happy news?" Benedetto said, shaking off the hold of two burly security guards before walking away of his own accord.

Engaged? Already?

Felipe ignored him.

"Shall we dance, Claudine?"

"That sounds nice. Please excuse us," she said to the wide-eyed people they'd been talking with.

Felipe cocked his head very briefly for a whisper from Vinicio before he waved Claudine to precede him.

Claudine pasted an unbothered smile on her lips and let him steer her toward the floor, but the harm was done. She could feel the sidelong looks.

Despite Felipe's impassive expression and the smooth way he guided her into the steps, she could feel the ire that radiated off him.

"Who is he?" she asked under her breath.

"No one. He raced the speedboat circuit with Francois and worked for the Italian Embassy until he was fired for misappropriation of funds. You'll never see him again. He must have been subbed in as a last-minute plus-one or he wouldn't have been allowed in."

"He's been a thorn in your side before?"

"I couldn't care less what my brother's cohorts say about me, but this salvo tells me Francois is unleashing his hounds on *you*, knowing full well I won't stoop to going after his own fiancée." A muscle pulsed in his jaw.

"Did you know about her? Who is she?"

"Vinicio just received the text. Princess Astrid, the daughter of a Danish prince. She was on Mother's short list." His mouth curled.

"She'll be pleased, then. Unlike how she feels about me." Claudine was starkly aware she fell far short in the Queen's estimation.

"You're not marrying her. You're marrying me." His firm hands pressed her back two steps before he gave her a slow twirl and brought her back into his arms.

It was the smallest gesture, but somehow she was breathless.

The dance ended and they left soon after.

As they entered their suite, he still wore tension across his cheekbones.

"I know what I said earlier, but I need to call the palace," he said.

"That's okay." All the travel and stress were catching up to her, leaving her yawning.

As she started into her room, he said, "Claudine. My bed is your bed."

She paused. "Is that an order or an invitation?"

"I thought it was what we both wanted. It's what *I* want."

Mollified, she said, "I was only going to my room to wash off my makeup and have Ippolita help me change."

His expression relaxed a fraction. "I won't wake you when I come to bed."

"You can," she said over her shoulder. "If you want to."

Some indeterminate time later, the mattress dipped and the covers stirred. She woke and rolled toward him, finding him naked.

"We don't have to. Are you tender from earlier?" He said that, but he was very hard and steely when she found his flesh beneath the covers.

"I want to. Can I try being on top?"

"You absolutely can, my beautiful treasure." He helped her slide the warm silk of her negligee up to her waist.

Claudine's mother had stayed behind in New York to make arrangements with her employer before coming to Nazarine. Felipe hired a nurse to assist her during the day as well as help her choose a specialist and make a plan for her ongoing care.

Claudine already missed her, but it was for the best that Ann-Marie didn't travel with them. Their commitments didn't stop once they left New York. They had engagements in several cities on their way back to Nazarine, attending meetings, dinners and appointments with every type of official including a lawyer who prepared their prenuptial agreement. Claudine also had more fittings and discussions with decorators along with interviews with staff.

Thankfully, their busy schedule meant they didn't see Francois until a few days before their wedding. The Spare had not been so lucky with gaining approval for his own wedding date. Given that his bride, Astrid, was a royal in her own right, she had initially asked for a year to plan their lavish wedding. They had settled on three months from now.

Francois was not hiding his resentment. He was quoted in the papers saying various unpleasant things about Claudine and Felipe and their own rush to the altar.

Claudine wished she could have avoided him indefinitely, but she was forced to attend a gala with the entire royal family where she finally came face-to-face with him for the first time since that horrible night on his boat.

She was standing with the King and Queen when she saw him approaching. She barely looked at his fiancée. Her heart had begun to beat wildly and she unconsciously stepped closer to Felipe.

His arm slid around her, firm hand closing on her waist while the rest of him remained relaxed but ready. His shuttered gaze watched his brother with undisguised contempt.

Felipe's lack of fear, and the calm reassurance he radiated that he would protect her, gave her the courage to stand tall and look Francois in the eye when he turned from greeting his parents.

"Felipe, you've met Princess Astrid. Claudine, I doubt you would have crossed paths with her." Because she was a commoner, his pithy tone implied. "Forgive me, but—"

Never, she thought, keeping her expression impassive.

"All the pageant girls blend together in my mind. Are you the one who never knew your father?"

"She's the one you lost," Felipe said starkly.

"Oh, goodness," Astrid interjected with the dulcet tone of someone well practiced in smoothing over a social conflict. "*I* know who *you* are. Patriotism had me rooting for our own contestant, but I thought you absolutely deserving of the win if that's how it panned out."

"That's kind of you to say," Claudine said sincerely, aware that Francois's remark had been loud enough to quiet the voices around them. She couldn't ignore it and didn't want to. "I know as much about my father as I need to," Claudine told him clearly. "Sadly, I lost my one mother when I was a child. My other one will arrive tomorrow for the wedding, however. I'm excited to show her around Sentinella. I think she'll find it very interesting."

"Has she never seen Alcatraz? Any Hollywood feature is enough to get the idea," Francois drawled.

"I've always found Sentinella very drafty," the Queen piled on. "Cold and unpleasant."

Claudine couldn't possibly contradict the Queen, not in public like this, but the more she had seen how irrevocably the Queen was on Francois's side, the more she felt it was a betrayal of Felipe, who was equally her son.

"Perhaps my mother would be more comfortable in your apartment at the palace?" Claudine suggested to Felipe, knowing full well the Queen would consider that even more intolerable. "We could stay with her there."

"Perhaps," he agreed, sliding his gaze to Claudine's so she saw the glitter of amusement in the depths of his irises.

His mother sent an icicle-laden stare at them while his father moved the conversation into more stately topics.

When she had an opportunity, Claudine sought the ladies' lounge. It was designed as a small oasis with a sitting area of comfortable chairs in rose-colored velvet. Full-length mirrors were strategically placed to ensure one could scrutinize for flaws at every angle. A door led into a well-appointed powder room, and an attendant hovered, eager to provide any mending, makeup repairs or medical aid.

Two women left as she arrived, so she had the lounge to herself, allowing her to take slow breaths and try to release some of the evening's strain from her nerve endings.

"Oh." Princess Astrid faltered as she entered and saw Claudine at the mirror. "This is a nice surprise. We haven't had a chance to say a proper hello, have we?"

"We haven't." Claudine twisted her lipstick back into its tube and dropped it into her clutch, trying not to feel inferior to her. It was hard, though, after listening to the Queen build up this woman all evening while barely acknowledging Claudine was alive. "Are you enjoying the evening?"

"I'm not sure," Astrid said wryly. "The rivalry between our respective grooms is more overt than I anticipated. I hope you and I will manage to be friends, though." She sounded sincere. Nice. Too nice for Francois.

"I hope so, too," Claudine murmured. "I'll give you your privacy."

As she reached the door, however, she knew she couldn't leave it at that.

"Would you excuse us?" Claudine asked the attendant who looked surprised, but stepped from the room and closed the door behind her.

Astrid looked up from the clutch she had opened.

"I could never call myself your friend unless I told you something you deserve to know," Claudine began.

They flew back to Sentinella for the night.

It was Claudine's first arrival back here since they had left for Paris and New York. As she stepped inside the high walls of the fortress, she felt as though a valve released and she could finally breathe.

She didn't realize it came out as a long sigh until Felipe said, "I feel the same way whenever I return."

Claudine had thought she was the only one to find the royal palace a nonstop pressure cooker of tension. It had been oppressive before she'd told Astrid what Francois had done to her. From that point on, the rest of the evening had been one of sick dread while she waited for the fallout.

She would have to tell Felipe she'd spoken to Astrid, she knew that, but she dreaded that, too.

Ippolita had been on the same helicopter and was following them through the snaking path toward Felipe's bedchamber.

"Thank you, Ippolita," Claudine paused to say in Italian. "I can manage. Have a good night."

"Nothing to eat?" Felipe asked. "You barely touched your plate at dinner."

"No. *Grazie*."

The maid murmured good-night and turned toward the stairs into the servants' quarters.

"Are you feeling ill?" Felipe asked as they entered the parlor next to his bedchamber.

"A little, but don't get your hopes up." She waited until he closed the door and glanced around to be sure they were alone. "I get this headache and backache every month."

"Ah. I thought you were gone from the ballroom an inordinately long time." He set aside the drink he'd been about to pour. "How bad is it? Shall I get you a pain pill?"

"I took one. You're not disappointed?"

"A little, but it's not something we can control, is it? What are you feeling? You're usually easier to read, but you seem…" He searched her expression. "I don't know. Are you upset?"

"I always get the blues on my first day. And the timing was wrong, so I didn't really expect it to work, but…" She was disappointed. Very. Which didn't make much sense except that she was excited for the idea of having a baby now that it had become a possibility. At the same time, having been subjected to all that coldness at the palace, she had to wonder if it wasn't a blessing that she wasn't pregnant. Did she really want to bring a baby into such a hostile environment?

"I don't know what to feel," she admitted.

"Look. Claudine." Felipe came to warm her upper arms with the light skim of his hands. "I know I've been pushing you where this marriage is concerned, but I am not a medieval monster. Please do not feel pressured to achieve something that is completely out of our hands. Aside from the obvious," he added dryly.

She nodded, appreciating him saying that since she did feel that conceiving a future king or queen was her primary purpose. Would he still want to marry her, though, after she told him what she'd done?

He had drawn her closer and she leaned into him, absorbing his strength, enjoying the warm hand that made soothing circles against her lower back.

"If you don't feel like making love, I completely understand," he said in a rumble. "I will even call Ippolita myself to run you a bath, if you'd like that."

She drew back and admonished him with an eye roll, since they were both perfectly capable of turning a tap, but his lips were twitching. He was teasing her. And cradling her very tenderly. She could have cuddled into him for the rest of the night.

"On the other hand, if you *would* like to make love, I am more than willing," he said with a light trace of his fingertip along her cheek. "No pressure. It's simply information I want you to have."

Why was he being so nice? It made what she had to say so much harder. She drooped her head against his shoulder, then made herself step out of his arms.

"I told Astrid."

"Told—? Ah." His whole demeanor changed, but she didn't get a chance to read his expression. He went to the bottle of brandy he had started to pour. "How did she react?"

"With suspicion and disbelief." Claudine hugged herself, trying to quell a grim sense of scorn and failure. Possibly the worst part was that she had known this was how it would go, yet she was profoundly stung it had gone that way anyway. "I told her I would never forgive myself if he hurt her in the future and I hadn't warned her, but Francois had already told her I would likely make trouble on your behalf, that I would throw out false accusations against him, so that's what she assumed I was doing."

"Did you tell her we have video evidence that you swam ashore? And Dr. Esposito's report?"

"According to Francois, I got myself banged up on a motor scooter and knew I would lose the pageant. I targeted you and you have helped me to fabricate evidence. Your interest in me is pure spite against him." She shouldn't be surprised by the lengths that man would go, but she had been shocked at Astrid's calm dismissal of all she'd said.

"So she plans to marry him anyway." He finally turned and regarded her over his half-raised glass, still unreadable.

"That's not why I told her. I wasn't trying to stop their marriage. That's her choice. I was only clearing my conscience and telling her something she deserves to know. I told her that if anything comes up in future, I'll believe her and support her any way I can. Are you angry?" She hunched her shoulders defensively, bracing herself for his answer. "Do you think I should have spoken up sooner? Publicly?"

"I'm always angry," he said in a tone that was grim but weary. "Especially at him." He lifted his gaze from the amber liquid he was swirling, revealing the bitter shadows that lurked behind his eyes. "I understand there is a cost to you whether you speak up or stay silent. I'm angry at *that*, but I try to focus on the things I can change." He threw back his drink. "And I appreciate that you tried, despite knowing that it might have no effect on her."

"Thank you," she said to the floor, kind of

touched even though she was also filled with despair. "I didn't know how you would react."

"With pride, Claudine."

His tone of quiet sincerity shook her apart inside, lifting a strange sensation of wonder and yearning behind her breastbone.

"I'll run you a bath." He walked away.

"Rhys," Felipe said as he entered the anteroom of the church. "Thank you for coming on such short notice."

"Felipe." Rhys Charlemaine, Prince of Verina, came forward to shake his hand. "I'm honored you asked. It's also an excellent excuse to sail your beautiful islands and show them to my wife."

"Cassiopeia is well? The rest of your family?" They were a similar age, so they had crossed paths at school and other events through the years. They had many things in common, not least the challenges of royal life and a similar approach to living it. In finding his bride, Rhys had managed to unearth a woman with royal lineage, but she had been raised in Canada in a very down-to-earth manner.

They caught up on the necessary small talk, then Rhys said, "I thought you might ask Francois to be your best man. Things are still less than ideal there?"

"Your diplomacy is as razor-sharp as always," Felipe said dryly.

"Some relationships are more difficult than others. I understand that. It's still unfortunate." Rhys maintained his circumspect tone and expression.

Felipe didn't think less of him for it. Politics could change in an instant. Personal remarks had to be kept as neutral as possible in their circles. Rhys knew that all too well. He had endured his own difficulties in his past, but he had always remained close with his older brother, King Henrik of Verina. The animosity between Felipe and Francois was incomprehensible to him.

"Relationships demand respect," Felipe said, thoughts leaping automatically to Claudine—as if she was ever far from the forefront of his mind. "I lost all of mine for my brother long ago."

In fact, Felipe had thought there was nothing Francois could do to sink lower in his estimation, but he had. The pageant winner had been announced a few days ago, along with the fact this would be the final Miss Pangea. When Francois was interviewed about that, he had fielded questions that were obvious setups to smear Claudine.

"What of the rumor that Miss Sweden was disqualified for ethics violations? Can you confirm that she left of her own volition? Or was she asked to leave?"

"For privacy reasons, I must decline to an-

swer," Francois had said with one of his patented looks of pained regret, making Felipe want to strangle him.

"I'm pleased to fill in," Rhys said magnanimously. "And Sopi asked me to invite you to visit us in Verina as soon as you have time." Sopi was his nickname for his wife. "She knows how overwhelming this can be and wants to be sure your bride knows she has friends."

"I'm sure Claudine would appreciate that. I'll have Vinicio liaise with your people."

Assistants entered with last-minute checks and the news that the bride had arrived. They were instructed to take their positions.

Felipe wouldn't admit to nervousness that Claudine would fail to appear at the altar, but the possibility had been there, especially since she wasn't yet pregnant.

That had hit him harder than he had expected, not that he'd shown it. It wasn't all because of this damned race against Francois, either. In the back of his mind, he'd always had the belief that if worst came to worst, and Felipe sat on the throne while Francois produced the next heir, Felipe would find a way to take custody of the future ruler himself. Because, among the many things that Francois should not be allowed to do, raising children was definitely one.

That was a turmoil best not started unless absolutely necessary, however. Thus, Felipe was marrying Claudine and planning to conceive his own heir with her.

Her innocence kept striking him, though. Her vulnerability. She hadn't said so openly, but he'd seen how upset she'd been that Astrid hadn't believed her. It was exactly what she had feared would happen if she came forward, but she had tried to protect Francois's bride anyway, suffering for the effort. Felipe had no doubt that Claudine's actions were the reason behind his brother taking special steps to muddy Claudine's reputation. It was retaliation.

Rhys had called their world overwhelming and it was, but Felipe's twin made it harrowing for Claudine. If he, Felipe, was a man with any true integrity or conscience, he wouldn't drag her further into it. He would protect her by pushing her as far away as possible from himself.

Maybe he would have, if the music hadn't already started and he hadn't looked up the aisle to catch sight of her.

His breath was punched out of him. She was a vision in ivory silk with a sheen that made her glow. She wore a tiara he'd gifted to her for this ceremony and she held her head high.

He couldn't look away from her. She seemed to hold his gaze the whole way down the aisle, escorted by her mother's slow gait. When she arrived before him, there were questions in her eyes.

He imagined she was wondering if she was doing the right thing. This was the final moment when she could back out, when he should have released her.

They both stayed exactly where they were, held as though by an invisible dome that formed around them, holding them in this moment.

He wanted her, he acknowledged. It had nothing to do with the crown or the future ruler or even the lust that had been simmering in his blood from the first time he clapped eyes on her.

This woman, whose hands settled on his open palms, filled him with more than pride. It was a force. Strength? Possessiveness? Reverence? It was a mix of all of those as well as an intense protectiveness that poured out of him to surround her. No one understood how truly remarkable she was, not the way he did. That was why he had to make her his.

Was it a rationalization to get what he wanted? Perhaps. But nothing in this world could have stopped him from claiming her right now.

So he did.

CHAPTER TEN

CLAUDINE HAD FALLEN into bed on arrival last night, exhausted by their long day. She woke as she often did these days, with the weight of Felipe's arm across her waist and the heat of his body spooned behind hers.

Her own arm was draped across his. Her seeking finger found the gold band she had placed on his hand yesterday. It was done. She was married to him.

Misgivings had chased her throughout the morning of her wedding, when her mother had asked her more than once, "Are you sure?"

The ceremony itself had been beautiful and lavish. She had truly felt like a princess in her gown and tiara. She had been emotional and, for a few moments during the ceremony, had felt bound to him. United. One.

After that, however, it began to feel like a play that was performed for an audience. Felipe had been contained and watchful. Triumphant even, when they had danced and Francois circled past with Astrid. Claudine had been forced to recognize their marriage was not a happily-ever-after. It was an expedient move by a determined man.

With time in such short supply in Felipe's schedule, they were only taking a short week for their honeymoon. They had arrived very late last night in Stockholm after stopping in Switzerland, where Claudine had seen her mother checked into a world-renowned clinic. There, a cutting-edge specialist had met with them and reassured her mother that she would get the help she desperately needed before she went home to New York.

For that, Claudine would marry Felipe a dozen times, but despite waking in a five-star presidential-suite bed, she was worried for her future. She had bound her life to a man she barely knew beyond the fact his family was as broken as they were blue-blooded. Felipe was powerful and driven and had done something invaluable for her mother, but only to achieve his own ends. He didn't love her. He didn't even believe in the emotion.

She did. Worse, she suspected, that was the reason she was here. She was falling for him despite his wall of cynicism. That scared her, because he was not a man who could be moved by anything but logic. Her heart could reach and stretch, but it would never touch his.

What had she done?

"You know I'm awake," he said in his morning-gruff voice, breath stirring her hair against her ear. "Do you want to make love?"

"Do you?" She realized she'd been tracing the bump of his wedding band all this time.

His scoffing noise chided her for having to ask when his erection was pressing the lace hem of her satin nightgown where it had ridden up against her buttocks. He shifted to loom over her and scrape his teeth against her bare shoulder.

She shivered and the yearning in her coiled toward arousal. This was why she had married him, because she only had to lie against him to become saturated with desire. When his body moved with light friction against hers, the flames caught. He opened his mouth against her nape and a delicate thrill ran down her spine, making her hips arch back in flagrant invitation.

With a growl of gratification, he reached up and over her to drag a pillow down, then used his lazy strength to roll her onto her stomach over it.

The covers fell away, sending cool air swirling around her, but she didn't care. She was already burning up.

"Bellissima." His thighs parted hers and his hands scraped up her hips, pushing the edge of the nightgown higher, baring her to his gaze.

She moaned, aware how shameless she was, but it didn't stop her from setting her hands against the headboard and offering herself to the hard flesh that stroked along her slick lips, strumming her flesh into vivid life before he sought entry.

They both released ragged groans as he drove into her. He was on his knees behind her, holding her hips steady for his powerful thrusts. It was raw and animalistic and she gloried in it.

This was why she had married him. This passion coupled with the sense that when they were like this, she gave him exactly what he gave her—utter pleasure. It was a potent aphrodisiac to meet his thrusts and reach to where they were joined and hear his breath change when her fingers brushed his flesh.

She loved most when they reached the pinnacle together. She could tell he was nearly there. So was she. It only took a light touch of her fingers against her most sensitized place and her inner flesh clamped onto his. Orgasm tumbled through her, sending her soaring and floating and…

He slowed his thrusts, moving strong and deep to prolong the convulsive waves that had her in thrall. When she was shaking and weak and still trying to catch her breath, he withdrew and rolled her off the pillow.

"Always so quick," he teased with lusty approval rasping his voice. "I love how greedy you are."

Her heart lurched, led one way by "I love," and yanked in another by the rest of what he'd said.

"I thought you were ready, too." It was disconcerting to realize he hadn't been nearly as aroused as she was.

"I'm greedy for *your* pleasure." He lowered his head to her breast and used his tongue to shift the lace against her nipple.

A fresh jolt of desire shot through her like electricity.

"Poor *cara mia*. Did you think I would do anything on our honeymoon beside make you mine in every possible way?" He slid his hand beneath the lace and exposed her breast, then dipped his head to take her naked nipple into his mouth.

It was a delicious, sensual assault that she couldn't help succumbing to, even as she realized that they might take equal pleasure in sharing their bodies, but he wasn't nearly so helpless to it as she was.

Felipe was a textbook case when it came to being a workaholic, so the annoyance he felt at the end of his honeymoon surprised him. Aside from daily visits to the gym and necessary meals, he worked constantly. Ski trips and other recreation were always combined with work. He had many responsibilities and they'd become heavier since his father's diagnosis.

It wasn't as if he would cease to see his wife, either. They made important appearances on their way home. And, while Claudine might eventually have a heavy calendar that conflicted with his own, it had become their habit to dine and sleep together. When he came out of meetings, she was never far if he wanted to find her.

This irritation with the intrusion of real life pressed guiltily against his conscience. He had been born to the crown, raised to wear it, and, for the sake of Nazarine, it was imperative that he continue to serve the throne. Any distraction from that was a threat to more than his sense of mental peace. It was a danger to the country that depended on him.

He had to remember that Claudine was a means to performing his duty. An extension of it, and nothing more.

His duty had never been such a pleasure, however, as when he escorted her into a charity gala in Portugal and she was introduced as his wife. She was beautiful. That went without saying, but she had the ability to make him catch his breath with a tilt of her smile or the feel of her long silk glove against his wrist.

His enjoyment of her presence beside him went beyond their sexual attraction and the boost to his male ego, too. He'd attended countless events like this with a woman on his arm. None had made him feel so…accompanied. That was it. In nearly every setting, he had always felt apart from the humanity around him, not that it had ever bothered him to be so, but with Claudine he was not alone in this sense of remoteness.

She didn't seem to feel the same removal, though. She shifted between the invisible spaces without effort or even awareness of it. She put people at ease and projected an air of warmth, then looked at him in a way that should have felt invasive, but was a welcome intrusion. Her clear alignment with him undid two decades of Francois's best attempts to label Felipe cold, corrupt and objectionable.

That amused Felipe no end, but he saw it as a liability, too, though. Being known as ruthless had its uses. Their romantic rush to the altar, dazzling as some found it, also made it seem as though he had a soft spot for her.

Seem? he chided himself. He *did* have one. His appearance of loving her offered her certain protections, but that same perception made it clear she was his Achilles' heel.

That concerned him. As much as he adored having her beside him, she created the sense of an unprotected flank. He didn't expect an attack to come from her, but she was not a shield. She was a crack where an attack could come through.

"Vinicio is trying to get your attention," she murmured when there was a break in the conversation they were having with a local dignitary.

"Excuse us," he said to the couple and brought her to where Vinicio offered his phone.

"A message marked *Private*, Your Highness, from Princess Astrid."

Felipe automatically held out his hand, but Vinicio said, "I beg your pardon, sir." He offered it to Claudine.

She took it with a blink of confusion, then her eyes widened as she read. She showed it to Felipe.

I believe you. He wanted to move up our wedding date and did not take it well when I resisted. I'm fine, but the wedding is off. I'm on my way home. I wanted to apologize for not believing you when you warned me about him. I really do hope we can be friends in future.

"Find out what's going on with Francois," Felipe instructed.

Vinicio took back his phone and brought it to his ear as he moved out of the ballroom.

"I guess we didn't need to marry quite so fast," Claudine said with a weak smile.

Her remark had him reaching out to catch at her gloved hand, as if he had to physically restrain her from walking away from him.

"He'll replace her very quickly."

Her brow tugged into a brief frown of agony. He swore under his breath as he heard her thoughts.

She would have to rake over her experience again and again, going through the process of being disbelieved again and again, as she continued to warn these other women.

Make a public statement, he wanted to insist, but clamped his lips tight. It had to be her decision.

"I think I expected to feel some kind of satisfaction or sense of vindication if she left him, but there's not," she said glumly.

"Shall we leave?" he asked.

"Only if you want to. I'm fine," she said with another wan smile.

Duty had him scanning the room for people he had yet to greet. It was the last thing he wanted to do or put her through. He was already wondering how Francois would choose to retaliate for this, but Felipe's desire to take her home only underscored how much she was impacting his ability to put his duty to the crown ahead of personal interests.

"Let me introduce you to the prime minister." He nodded at a hovering assistant who hurried to make it happen.

After a whirlwind of appearances, they finally returned to Nazarine and the blissful serenity of Sentinella.

Home, Claudine thought, as Felipe rolled his naked body away from hers.

They had enjoyed a lazy morning of lengthy lovemaking, but now he said, "I have meetings with my father all afternoon. You're welcome to come to the palace with me, but you don't have to."

"Honestly, if I could browse the shops on Stella Vista without creating a scene, I would." She mourned the simple freedoms of her old life sometimes. "Your parents don't expect me, do they?"

"No, this is purely business with my father."

"I'll stay here, then."

"And keep my bed warm?"

"And call my mother." Ann-Marie's most recent messages had been upbeat. The new clinic was trying some advanced therapies that seemed to have halted this latest spiral, and some of her symptoms seemed to be less severe. "Maybe I'll check in with Astrid, too."

Claudine had sent her a brief note, telling her she would also like to be friends and had promised to connect properly as soon as she had a moment.

Felipe kissed her, then rose to shower. He was gone within thirty minutes, swearing that the sooner he left the sooner he'd be back.

He was back a lot sooner than Claudine expected. She had only had time to shower and eat a late breakfast. She was sitting by the fountain inside the maze, contemplating whether to make a public statement about Francois, when she heard the helicopter.

Felipe appeared before she had walked more than halfway out.

"What's wrong?" she asked across the zigzag of boxwood.

"He found your father," Felipe said grimly.

Francois hadn't released the story himself, of course. He had used one of his scandal sheet contacts to blast across the headlines that the new Princess of Nazarine had been conceived by a man who had died of an illicit drug overdose years ago.

Felipe didn't care about such details himself, no matter how sordid the reporters tried to make it sound, but he was livid that Claudine was upset by it—not that she was concerned for herself.

"His poor family. Does he have any? I should call my mother. How is the palace taking this?"

The palace, his own pathetic family, were expressing "concern" and "looking into it." They did absolutely nothing to punish Francois for violating Claudine's privacy. Felipe's meeting with his father had been a short, snarling few words demanding he put his brother in his place.

"You're turning a blind eye to his sullying the royal family like this? Again?"

"She's not family, is she? And she fired her own shots across his bow by badmouthing him to Astrid."

"She told the *truth*," Felipe had roared before

climbing straight back into his helicopter to come here and tell Claudine.

She finished up her conversation with her mother. They signed off with their standard, "Love you."

"Love you, too."

That always gave him a strange sensation when he heard that. Envy? He shook it off.

"How is she?" he asked grimly.

"Concerned about how I was taking it," Claudine said, mouth quivering with emotion.

"And? How are you taking it?" Felipe prodded, aware that she had been so upset for others she hadn't expressed her own feelings on the matter.

"Honestly? I'm really sad that he's not still alive. That breaks my heart." Her eyes were bright with unshed tears. "I've always held on to a small hope I might meet him someday. Now that it will never happen, I'm deflated. And I hate that Francois is exploiting him this way when he can't even defend himself."

"It's reprehensible." Felipe drew her into his arms, trying to offer what comfort he could, but his conscience tortured him. "I never should have pulled you into the ring of my fight with my brother."

"He and I fought before you and I had ever met," she reminded him, drawing back enough to look into his eyes. "I'm sorry that you have had a lifetime of fighting with him. Of never knowing what it is to have family who loves and supports you. I can't imagine how hard that's been for you."

Such a wrenching sensation went through his chest that he nearly mistook it for a medical event. He swallowed back the profound ache and held her closer, tucking her face into his shoulder so she wouldn't see how completely she had leveled him with her wish that he had experienced something he had long ago convinced himself he didn't need.

"Don't worry about me," he insisted gruffly. "I want to know how I can help you."

"I don't think there is anything that can help. I presume if he had family, they would have been identified already."

"I asked Vinicio to investigate—" He cut himself off as there was a knock at the door.

Felipe dropped his arms so they both faced his secretary as Vinicio entered with the closest thing to excitement he had ever exhibited.

"Sir. I think this could be positive news."

There was no reason for Felipe to feel a level of threat this intense. It wasn't physical, which was probably why it was so uncomfortable. His team had verified everything, so traveling to Sicily carried virtually no risk to either of them.

Emotionally, however, there was the potential for great jeopardy.

Felipe had trained himself to avoid emotions. The ones he allowed himself to feel were generally the ones surrounding his brother's behavior and even those bouts of fury and bitterness he routinely watered down and ignored.

He didn't allow himself the folly of hope or joy. Never ever the hope *for* joy.

There was Claudine beside him, though, drying her palms on the raw silk trousers she wore, chewing her lip, fairly quivering with anticipation of something that could turn out to be profoundly disappointing.

How was he supposed to protect her from that? He couldn't.

Which churned an unfamiliar helplessness in his gut, but he couldn't deny her this chance, could he? Not when she had told him how much she had clung to the hope that she might one day meet the man who'd made her. This wasn't that, but it was the next best thing.

The helicopter flight was just over an hour. They landed on a private estate where two of Felipe's guards greeted them, having come in this morning to ensure everything was as secure as promised. The pair fell into step with them as they were escorted down a wide, paved path toward a beautiful single-level villa.

As the path brought them into a garden where

a freeform swimming pool gleamed in the midday sun, a family waited to greet them.

Freja, Claudine's cousin, was a blonde woman closing in on thirty. She resembled Claudine even more in person than in her photos. It went beyond the physical into the warmth she radiated and the gleam of liveliness in her eyes.

Her husband, Giovanni, looked closer to forty. He gave off a relaxed air, but there was a quiet suggestion of power in his wide shoulders and watchful gaze. Their twin girls were three years old and stood wide-eyed on either side of their father's wheelchair, each clutching a posy of flowers.

As one of the assistants provided introductions, and the men reached to shake hands, the girls hurried forward to thrust their small bouquets at Claudine.

"Thank you. *Grazie.*" Claudine crouched to take them, looking deeply moved. "Which one of you is Louisa and—"

"She's Theresa, I'm Louisa," one said hurriedly.

"Where's your crown?" Theresa asked with a worried look at Claudine's hair.

"They don't wear them every day, angel." Freja gave her daughter's fine hair a tender smooth. "I hope you don't mind." Freja bit her lip against helpless laughter. "They wanted to meet a real princess."

"*I* wanted to meet a real cousin and look at you both! I swear I have a photo of myself at your age that looks just like you two." She was blinking back tears of joy.

"I would love to see it," Freja said, then urged the girls, "Off you go with nanny. I'll call you when it's time to say goodbye."

The girls were pulled away and Giovanni invited them to sit in a shaded settee near the pool. Refreshments were served, but Felipe didn't think Claudine noticed anything beyond her newly discovered cousin. She was staring and smiling at Freja and Freja did the same thing back, both seeming nearly speechless with happiness.

"I must apologize for the way this news came out," Felipe said, prepared to offer a more thorough explanation, but Freja held up a hand.

"Please. I'm very used to publicity." Freja's father had been a famous travel writer. She had toured the world with him and developed her own following after writing a book about him. More recently she had released a documentary on her life with him.

Perhaps what she was really most known for, however, was the fact that her husband had been presumed dead some years ago. Yet he was alive and well today, affably pouring wine that appeared to be from their personal vineyard.

"I'm far too thrilled to meet my cousin to let

the way I found out tarnish it," Freja continued. "I always knew my father's brother had donated sperm to a clinic. It actually gave my father a lot of comfort, believing that something of his brother possibly lived on, but it seemed impossible that I would ever get the chance to meet any children he helped to make. It wasn't on my radar at all. Not until Giovanni told me this morning that—" She looked to her husband, appearing unsure how much to say.

"Given Freja's high profile, I have robust on-line alerts set around her name and those of any connections that might crop up," Giovanni said smoothly, as though it hadn't been a needle in a haystack for him to have put this together that fast. "Freja's father wrote about his brother in this book." He reached into the carry-all pocket that hung off his chair. "There are some photos of him, too. I've marked it. Freja thought you'd like to have it."

"Giovanni knows my father's books better than I do," Freja said with a self-deprecating grimace. "But I have other copies, so please keep that one."

"This means the world to me. Thank you." Claudine hugged the book. "What else can you tell me about him?"

"Not much, I'm afraid. I was still very young when my uncle died. I don't have any memories of him at all. You'll be able to tell that my father adored him and missed him all the rest of his life." She nodded at the book. "I remember him talking about Uncle Leif as someone who was endlessly curious, but never stuck with anything for long. He was more interested in the challenge and, once he learned all he needed to, he jumped into something else. He hated to lose any sort of game, whether it was checkers or even solitaire."

"Oh?" Claudine glanced at Felipe, mouth twitching ruefully.

"They were supposed to go traveling together, but my father married my mom and had me. Uncle Leif then planned to go alone, but the night before he left, he went to a rave and took some party drugs that turned out to be toxic. Don't believe what was said online. If he'd been a longtime user of heavy drugs, he wouldn't have been allowed to donate to the clinic. This was a one-time thing that turned out tragically."

"Very tragic," Claudine agreed, mouth tilting downward with sadness.

"The reports around the circumstances of his death will be corrected, I assure you," Felipe promised.

"My team is already on it," Giovanni said. "You and I should discuss messaging. Let the women get to know each other and we'll take this to my office."

Felipe was surprised by that, but after one brief

glance at Claudine, who nodded and immediately turned back to Freja, he rose and followed Giovanni into the villa.

An hour quickly passed. Talking to Freja was like talking to an old friend. Or, more specifically, to a close cousin she'd known all her life. It was remarkable.

When it was time to leave, she and Freja promised to keep in touch and hugged warmly. That signaled the girls to also give Claudine a hug. Claudine fought fresh tears all the way back to Sentinella.

"You haven't said much," Felipe noted when they entered the privacy of his office there. "Are you all right?"

"I'm so happy I feel like I owe Francois a thank-you card."

"Ha!" Felipe barked.

She bit her lip, always pleased when she could get a laugh out of him. If it was at his brother's expense, that was even better.

"I suppose I could say the same," he said dryly. "Here I thought you came without valuable connections. As it turns out, your cousin's husband is a lot more than the domestic family man he portrays himself to be."

"You didn't get that from his billion-dollar mansion and the mystique around his faked death?

What did you talk about when you two went inside?" she asked curiously.

"Things I'm not at liberty to repeat, but he is *very* well connected. He's also under no illusions as to Francois's true nature." He narrowed his eyes, staring thoughtfully into the middle distance.

"Freja said her PR team has already begun correcting my father's image. She said I'll soon have an army of her father's 'travel bugs' supporting me." That had made her laugh.

"Giovanni said something along the same lines."

"I liked them."

"Me, too."

Claudine paced a few steps, pensive. "I can't help thinking Francois will look for some other way to attack me now that this route hasn't worked." It was causing her some dread. And a spark of rage. She was so tired of being Francois's chosen victim. "I think it's time."

"Time?"

"To tell my story." As she said it aloud, she felt the rightness of it.

Felipe's mouth pressed into a line, but he nodded once, jerkily. "How would you like to go about it?"

CHAPTER ELEVEN

FELIPE BROUGHT IN his legal team. After a long consultation, Claudine took their advice to lodge a complaint of negligence and harassment against the pageant, since the corporation had yet to be dissolved. Claudine had been a resident of New York when she entered the contest and that was where the pageant headquarters were located, so that was where everything would be filed.

The timing worked with her mother. Ann-Marie would never fully recover the mobility or vision that she had recently lost in one of her eyes, but she was stable and proceeding with a new treatment plan that seemed to be keeping her feeling as well as possible. She was ready to go home to New York where Felipe had a team standing by to help her close up her apartment and move to a new building with better security and a live-in helper.

According to the press release that Felipe arranged, Claudine was assisting her mother with all of that. She was her mother's liaison with all the workers, but she also swore her statements while she was there.

On her return, Felipe met with his father to warn him that charges against Francois were likely.

"Why the hell did you let it get that far?" the King snarled.

"I told you when I chose Claudine that I would let her dictate when and how she told her story."

"And I allowed you to marry her believing you would quash it," Enzo thundered. "You're supposed to be making less work for me, not more. Have her withdraw her accusations."

"No." Felipe wasn't surprised by his father's reaction. He wasn't even angry. He was revolted. "This isn't a scandal. It's harassment and assault that could go much further than Francois. Other people could have been taking advantage of contestants. Do you really want to protect all of those abusers?"

His father muttered a number of overripe curses.

"It will take a few weeks for the charges to be filed. Claudine's statement will be released at that time. Don't bother using your connections to stop it," Felipe warned. "She'll go to the press regardless."

"You couldn't wait until you'd made an heir?

Your brother is next in line," his father spelled out as though Felipe was a child without the faculties to understand. "Think about that before you dishonor his name."

"He dishonors this country," Felipe insisted grimly. "How do you not see that?"

"He's all we have until you do your duty." The King smashed his fist onto his desktop. "Tell your mother." Enzo seated himself at his desk in the way he did when he was being as rudely dismissive as possible.

"Francois can tell her himself when he's indicted," Felipe muttered and walked out.

It was a tense time made worse by the fact Claudine discovered—again—that she wasn't pregnant. At least, she had a bit of spotting that ruined her day, making her believe she wasn't, but it disappeared by the next, which was confusing.

"What does that mean?" Felipe asked with a frown of concern.

"I don't know," she muttered truculently. "That I'm putting too much pressure on myself? I think it was the trip to New York. It feels like an ax waiting to fall."

He had told her how things had gone with his father over her statement. Claudine understood the urgency to create an heir, even though she knew that letting the pressure get to her wasn't helpful.

"One day at a time," Felipe murmured, rubbing her back. She knew he didn't blame her for Francois's behavior or their lack of conception, but guilt dogged her like a black cloud.

Her failure to conceive certainly wasn't for lack of trying, she thought dourly. They made love as often as possible despite how busy they were. Over the next weeks, they flew to Berlin and Hong Kong, then came back by way of Cairo, which was fascinating, but hot. She caught a glimpse of the pyramids from the airplane, but otherwise it was nothing but parading in gowns and talking business.

She didn't mind the travel and small talk. She was meeting interesting people, but the only time she seemed to connect with her husband was in bed—where they made love in a pleasured frenzy. Any words they exchanged were sexual, never emotional or personal.

It was frustrating. She wanted...something. Some indication that she meant more to him than the vessel for an heir. Was this all they would ever have between them? Sex and the stratagems of her statement? Because she was feeling very trapped in a prison of her own making.

She was in the library, trying to recall which books he had moved to make the wall open, but it wasn't working. She was frustrated and feeling stymied and blocked. Not imprisoned, but held by an invisible force, one she couldn't name.

She didn't *want* to name it. To name it was to succumb to it in all its vast glory.

And to recognize that she was alone in feeling this way.

"Oh, Claudine," she chided herself exactly as her mother might do if she forgot to study or lost her keys or signed up for a pageant even though her mother had expressly asked her not to.

Because what she'd done was go and fall in love with her husband—fathoms deep in love. Which wasn't a crime. Not by any means. It simply wasn't wise.

What was she supposed to do now?

She heard the helicopter return, signaling he was back from his latest meetings with his father. She stayed in the library, not even turning when the sound of approaching footsteps arrived behind her with a blast of crackling energy.

"You're back early." She didn't turn to face him. Did this one go in? She kept searching for evidence on the shelf, a rail of dust or a fingerprint, but she couldn't find any hints to help her.

"Your lawyer has filed the charges." The door closed. "Francois will be notified shortly, but the statements to the press won't release until after my parents' anniversary party."

"Francois will know, though," she repeated,

feeling the invisible clock ticking down. Three more days and the details of her dark night in the water would be known by all. "Will his new fiancée be there?"

"Yes."

Eloise was the daughter of a British duke. So far, Eloise had only met the King and Queen. At least, Claudine wouldn't have to muster up her courage for a heart-to-heart with her. Her accusations would be all over the headlines the following day.

"What are you doing?" Felipe's voice was directly behind her.

"Trying to remember how to open the secret passage. Queen Giulia could have escaped. She could have seduced a captain and sailed away. Why didn't she?"

"Her children were here. They had entitlements that would have been lost if she took them away from Nazarine. And she knew she had more power inside these walls than out. Why? Are you trying to escape me?" His hand covered hers, moving it down two books and withdrawing one spine.

"Perhaps I'm trying to let my lover in." She was being metaphoric, but also deliberately provocative, wondering if she could get a reaction out of him, even if it was lowly jealousy.

"Your lover is already here, Your Highness." Her skin tightened with delight, but there was that other, anxious piece that had her stiffening slightly as he closed his hands on her upper arms.

He stilled. "No?"

"I—" She reflexively pushed her bottom back into his groin and instantly felt the thickness of his erection. Mindless passion was no substitute for love, but it fed something in her to know that he wanted her as badly as she wanted him. "H-here?"

"Right here, if that's what you want."

"I do," she whispered.

"Then hold on to this shelf." He guided her hands to the one in front of her eyes.

His touch trailed under her arms and down her rib cage. One hand swept forward to gather her breast through the silk blouse she wore. His body bowed around hers and his other palm slid to press the pleats of her skirt against her mound so she felt the strong flex of his hand there, *claiming*.

She writhed in the trap of his arms, stimulating both of them with the rock of her hips.

His mouth bypassed the hair she had clipped low behind her neck and his teeth scraped against her nape. With the light pinch of his fingers through her bra stinging her nipple, and the relentless pressure of his hand between her legs, she quickly grew aroused.

"Who are you?" she gasped. "A pirate? A smuggler?"

His head abruptly lifted and he slowly turned her. His hand dragged at her hair. "Look at me."

She forced her eyes open to see something atavistic in his gaze. Possessive? Threatened?

"I am your husband. Your future king. The only lover you will ever need."

His command for recognition lit something in her. A fierce compulsion to break past this wall between them and reach him. Without thinking, she clasped his head and brought his mouth down to crush her own against it, then speared her tongue into his mouth.

He gave a grunt of surprise, then tried to take control of their wild kiss, but she refused to allow it. She closed her fingers in his hair and arched against him blatantly, deliberately trying to incite him past his usual restraints. He always took her apart so easily. For once, she wanted to know she could do the same to him.

She loved him and it was eating her alive.

She pushed her hand between them, squeezing his shape through his trousers before delving behind his belt and past the constriction on his boxer briefs to the thick flesh that pulsed as she closed her fist around him.

His breath hissed in and his nostrils twitched.

"Why the hurry, *cara mia*?" He held her bold stare as she caressed him, trying to make him break.

She almost had him. She could see the effort it was costing him to keep his narrowed eyes open. His jaw was clenched, his breaths unsteadily. There was a slippery dampness against her thumb that she rolled around and around his tip, causing him to grow even harder in her grip.

"What is your end game?" he asked in a rasp.

"Why do you think this is a game?"

"Because I can see you are trying to win, *cara mia*. What do you want? To break me? You can try." He opened his belt and fly so her hand easily slipped free when he shifted her backward, causing her to stumble.

He caught her, of course, and pressed her to the narrow, cushioned bench of the reading nook. The high sun splashed down onto her, blinding her, but she didn't need to see when she could feel her skirt being flicked up to her waist and his knee parting her thighs.

And she thought, *Damn you. I will break through to you.*

She blinked against the sharp glare. He was a backlit shadow looming over her, but she halted him from kissing her by catching her fingers between the buttons of his shirt. She wrenched it open so a button pecked her cheek as it flew off. Then she splayed her hands across his naked chest and pressed her thumbs to the sharp points of his nipples.

"Oh?" With one hand, he did the same to her

top, yanking it so roughly, the silk tore and hung off her side, baring her bra. He shoved aside the lacy cup, exposing her breast.

Did he think that would disconcert her? She reached down and pulled her underwear to the side, further exposing herself. She caressed herself, parting and preparing herself. Beckoning and teasing and daring him to take her.

His fierce gaze raked down her torso and lower. His expression wasn't so much possessive or aggressive as *exalted*. As though he had discovered something wondrous. His brow flexed and his mouth tightened with strain. It was taking everything in him to hold on to his control.

That was when she saw him. She saw the beast and the man and the war between them. He didn't trust that beast, so he kept him caged.

The funny thing was, she did trust that animal. She recognized him as her mate and knew he would never hurt her.

That realization caused a strange mix of tenderness and wanton abandon to overtake her. She opened her bra and brought her knee up, inviting him to hook her foot onto his shoulder.

"I am your wife. Your future queen. *Yours.* Take me."

The rush of his breath was the sound a bull might make before it charged. He brushed aside his clothing and braced a hand above her shoulder, pinning her hair as he entered her in one implacable thrust.

Joyous tingles swept up from her loins through her whole body, filling her with gratification as he withdrew and returned, landing even harder and deeper.

"You *are* mine." He hugged her thigh and moved with uncontained power. "Look at me. Say it."

She could hardly make her eyes open, too overwhelmed by the thrill of pushing him right to the edge.

"You are mine," she taunted with a wicked smile.

His back flexed as though he'd been lashed and his teeth bared, but he didn't stop claiming her with those formidable thrusts of his hips. Each impact of his pelvis to hers caused every nerve in her body to sing, but he moved his hand between them, caressing to increase her pleasure even more.

She knew what he was doing, though. He was trying to push her past her limit, trying to make her break first.

Rather than try to best him, she took the advice he had given her the first time he had touched her so intimately. She cupped her own breasts and threw back her head and moaned to the high ceiling as she reveled in the powerful orgasm that soared upward, throwing her into the clouds.

He swore sharply and lost his rhythm. His hips

crashed once more into hers and they were both convulsing in the pulses and throbs of a powerful climax.

When he swore again, it was with defeat. His weight sagged onto her and she cradled his head, finally understanding.

He kept that wounded, angry part of himself walled off to preserve his own sanity. To love him was to climb into that cage with that beast and he would never allow it.

She sifted his hair through her fingers, looking to the ceiling with equal parts yearning and despair.

Three days ago, Felipe had gone back to Sentinella with a sense of urgency snapping at his heels. Or rather, with a sense that something was slipping through his grasp.

Through the course of his life, he had carefully constructed his world in a way that was not unlike the meditation maze. Anyone who wished to get close to him had to work through layers of backtracking to even come close. It was the defense mechanism that allowed him to cope with his father's indifference to him as a human being, with his mother's cold rejection of him in favor of his brother, and with his brother's open aggression.

He trusted no one absolutely and cared only a superficial amount for those who were allowed close to him.

Then Claudine had fought her way onto his island. He had carried her himself into his stronghold. Into his bed.

Was it the sex? Was that why he was so infatuated and obsessed? If so, he was no better than an adolescent getting his first taste of passion.

It went so much further than that, though. She was constantly on his mind. He weighed every decision he made against how it would affect her and, when he had picked up the message that the charges had been filed, a sense of dread had accosted him. The train had left the station. There was no stopping it now.

His father was already furious and his mother's appalled resentment was a given. He had no feelings whatsoever for Francois's reaction, except perhaps satisfaction that he was being forced to face the consequences of his actions.

No, the cloying angst within him was solely for Claudine. What would this mean for *her*? And would all this fallout cause her to pull away from him? He deliberately held her at arm's length, but that was as far as he would let her go. He needed her within reach.

He needed *her*.

That was terrifying, but it had driven him back to Sentinella to find her playing with the wall, talking of leaving and taking other lovers. Her teasing had clawed into a raw place inside him, stripping him of his usual patience and finesse.

Their lovemaking was often intense and primal, but that day in the library had been different. She had provoked him, yes, but a type of desperation had been driving him. A need to be inside her that had nothing to do with making the baby they were mandated to conceive and everything to do with binding her to him.

He stood on a knife's edge of wanting to be an absolute barbarian who chained his wife to his bed to ensure she was always with him and the civilized man who knew that was utterly mad.

They were married. That ought to be enough, but it wasn't. He couldn't help thinking that, at some point, she would come to her senses and leave him. And there was not one damned thing he'd be able to do about it.

"More bribery?" she admonished as she came out of their bedroom here at the palace. It was the King and Queen's anniversary celebration tonight. Possibly his father's last public appearance. "I didn't think I needed more sparkle, but I guess I was wrong."

She wore a shimmering gown covered in iridescent sequins. A mesh ruffle at the neckline glinted with crystals, but the diamonds from her ears dripped like icicles in the sunlight. The tennis bracelet on her arm was six rows wide.

"Thank you." She blinked the sooty lashes that

fanned below the silver shadow on her eyelids and pursed her glossy lips.

"You look stunning," he told her, feeling a pinch behind his heart as he touched his mouth to the corner of hers.

Mine, he thought yet again, and wanted to put his hands on her, as if that was all it would take to ensure she was always his.

"You look nice, too." She slid her fingertip along his satin lapel, then searched his gaze. "Is everything all right?"

"My mother has been informed." Or so Vinicio had told him a moment ago.

"Ah. Are we worried?"

"No. The news won't break into headlines until tomorrow. We'll get through one last, civilized evening." That felt like a lie, but he was only trying to keep her from fretting.

"I'm sorry that this makes your relationship with them that much more difficult," she said anxiously.

"Don't," he commanded gruffly. "*They* make it difficult." She made it bearable.

He took a moment to appreciate that. To bask in the light that was the pureness of her soul. It hurt the way bright sunlight hit the backs of his eyes, making them ache.

"Felipe?" She searched his expression, but he wasn't ready to pick apart what was happening to him.

He offered his arm and escorted her to the top of the grand staircase where they were announced right before the King and Queen followed them down.

The evening progressed as these things usually did. They mingled for an hour before the formal call to the dining hall. They were seated apart from one another, but Claudine was across from him at the table.

Two hundred guests were attending. An army of servants began to fill glasses and set the first of twelve courses. The din of conversation was near deafening, but settled each time someone gave a speech. Felipe stood to offer one. Francois gave another.

Claudine rose after the fish course, sending Felipe a look that was both apologetic and fretful before she walked away. He watched for her return, growing concerned when a quarter hour passed and she was still absent.

Francois's fiancée was still here at the table. Claudine wasn't tied up speaking to her.

Felipe looked to his brother and discovered Francois was staring at him. His brother wore a smug curl at the corner of his mouth.

Felipe's heart lurched.

Even as he started to rise, Vinicio was leaning to say in his ear, "Ippolita has called an ambulance. Her Highness is very ill."

CHAPTER TWELVE

DESPITE BEING SO violently ill that she was certain she would die, Claudine woke in the royal wing of the Stella Vista hospital.

Felipe stood over her, unshaven, eyes sunken into dark pools of brooding anger. He wore his tuxedo shirt open at the throat, his bow tie and jacket abandoned somewhere.

"How do you feel?" he asked in a voice that rasped across her dulled nerves. He gently brushed his fingertips along her jaw.

"What happened?" Her voice floated across the dry creek bed of her throat.

"You were poisoned. Francois is the culprit, not that I have proof. Now you're awake, I'll go to the palace to oversee the interrogations myself." He took out his phone and glanced at it. "Your mother has landed. She'll be here shortly."

He was avoiding her gaze, mouth tense. She had no doubt he was upset on her behalf, but all his emotions seemed to be directed at the palace and his brother. She couldn't discern how he felt beyond that. How he felt about *her*.

If he had told her in these moments that he loved her and was frightened for her and was grateful she had pulled through, she might have had a different reaction besides despair. As it was, all she could think was that even if he found the servant who had tainted her food, Francois would still be protected.

"For now, the pregnancy is unaffected."

As she gasped, his gaze slammed into hers. Inside those dark depths, she read shame and fierce protectiveness, helplessness and agonized yearning. That was why he was avoiding looking at her. She had nearly lost a baby she hadn't even known she carried!

"They did a blood test." His hand squeezed hers, perhaps reminding her to breathe because she suddenly realized she had no oxygen in her lungs.

She made herself shakily hiss air through her nostrils.

"I'm sorry, Claudine. I'm sorry it's come to this." His brows flexed in torture. "It never will again. I swear that to you."

All she could think was that if Francois had the means to slip her poison, he could dose her with a medication to end a pregnancy. She would never be safe! Neither would any child she had. Felipe would have to stay on guard forever, never allowing himself to love her or their child because he would be too afraid of losing both of them.

"I wouldn't leave you right now if I didn't have to," Felipe continued gently. "You understand that, don't you?" He rested his hand atop her head, looking so anguished it hurt to see it. "I have to go to the palace and finish this."

He did care for her, in his way, which meant she would hurt him when she did what she had to do, but it was the only way. She couldn't stay here and be the instrument his brother used to persecute him.

"I know," she murmured. "Can I have my phone?"

"Of course." His hand squeezed her limp fingers once more before he pressed her phone into it. "Your guards are right outside the door. You're completely safe." He leaned down to touch his mouth to her forehead. "Text me if you need anything at all."

She nodded and watched him leave before she texted Freja.

Claudine was a fighter.

Felipe had spent a long, dark night clinging to that knowledge while accepting that he could not ask her to be part of his fight any longer. Not if it might cost her her life.

A sense of déjà vu had gripped him as he stood over her, except that three months ago, he had seen her as a very useful pawn. Now he was ashamed to have pushed her into such a dangerous position, especially when she had come to mean so much to him. More than anyone else in the world. That was what he had acknowledged as he finally watched her blink her eyes open, only for fear and confusion to come into her pallid face.

And a baby? He couldn't even process that. Not yet. Not when Francois's actions could have taken both of them in the blink of an eye.

Leaving her had physically hurt, especially when paparazzi surrounded the hospital, clamoring at the news that had broken overnight about her accusations against Francois. It was an absolute nightmare, but once Felipe knew she was conscious, and would have her mother on hand, he *had* to come to the palace to deal with this once and for all.

Predictably, his father was uninclined to do what needed to be done.

"The culprit has been identified and is in custody," King Enzo said dismissively. "He claims to have acted out of spite toward America."

The King was gray beneath his normally swarthy complexion. It wasn't only the toll of a difficult night. His illness was beginning to run him down.

Felipe steeled himself against pitying him. He had never been shown such a thing by this man. "You really believe that? For God's sake, think of the damage he could do if he took the throne. Do you want that?"

"It doesn't matter what I want, Felipe. Francois is the spare." He whirled away in frustration. "I cannot believe I'm still having this conversation with you. Work it out! You're not children."

"You dare say that to me?" Felipe barely kept his grip on his temper. "When you have pitted us against one another our entire lives? No, we are not children. This is not a case of my brother stealing my favorite toy. *He tried to kill my wife. She's pregnant.* That is an attempted assassination of a future ruler."

"Is she?" King Enzo took a moment to absorb that, then, "Once she delivers—"

"No," Felipe roared. "Now. We take action *now.*"

There was an urgent knock, then Vinicio entered with a wild look in his eyes.

"I am deeply sorry, Your Majesty. Your Highness..." He dipped his head as he hurried toward Felipe. "A helicopter has just landed on the hospital's pad. It's from Sicily. The Princess appears to be boarding it with her mother."

If the blades had sliced and diced him into pieces, Felipe could not be more torn apart. For a few seconds, his entire being was incinerated by this news. By rejection. Loss. Scalding urgency rose in his chest with commands for her to be stopped, but he steeled himself against the searing pain and cleared his throat.

"Let her go." They were the hardest words he'd ever said, but a blinding truth arrived with them. She did not want to be married to the man he would have to become.

Vinicio hurried out to relay the message.

"You're allowing her to leave you?" his father scoffed. He blinked once, then turned his face away as though too filled with contempt to look at his son.

"You want me to keep her here where Francois can continue attempting to kill her? He has to be stopped," Felipe demanded. "If you don't have the stomach to deal with him, then give me the power to do so."

"Step down? No," Enzo said flatly.

"Then I'll do it my way." A sensation had arrived in Felipe, one he didn't know how to name. It wasn't vengeance or scorn or anything like the ugly bitterness he'd carried all his life. It was a clear, chilly calmness. Resolve.

He wasn't being honorable in releasing Claudine. He was setting aside his selfish desire to meld her to his side like an extension of himself. Instead, he would do what was necessary to ensure she lived a long, safe, happy life—even if it cost him his own.

Opening the door to his father's outer office, where a handful of assistants were going about their duties, he called, "Vinicio. Tell Francois to put his affairs in order and meet me in the courtyard at dawn."

Like in most Western countries, dueling with swords had fallen out of popularity in the kingdom once pistols were invented. Nazarine had very strict gun laws, some dating back to those early days of muskets and the like, in an effort to curb the practice, but dueling with swords had never been criminalized.

Thus, when Felipe threw down his gauntlet very publicly, promising the winner would take the throne, there was nothing to stop Francois from accepting except cowardice.

First, he tried labeling Felipe an unstable sociopath, but Felipe had only one response.

"Does that mean you forfeit?"

Francois did not. He showed up in the palace courtyard at dawn the following morning. Vinicio spoke to Francois's assistant long enough to explain that they could settle this without a fight if Francois gave up his right to the throne and left Nazarine forever.

"I would rather die," Francois called across the courtyard when his second relayed the terms.

"I can make that happen," Felipe assured him.

"You forget who wears the scar from our last duel. Have you held a sword since?"

Had Francois? To the best of Felipe's knowledge, neither of them had. Even back when they had learned to fence, the training foils had been blunt enough that a strike to an unprotected face would result in a bruise, not a cut.

Their instructor, however, had buckled to Francois's pleas and allowed the pair of *schiavonas*, antique cut-and-thrust swords, to be taken off the wall for their inspection.

A pair of guardsmen brought those same swords now, each in its leather scabbard, with the scrolled, polished steel of their basket-style hilts visible. A bright jewel glinted in each pommel.

"Stop this," the Queen ordered as she came outside in plain breakfast dress and a knitted cardigan. "You're making a mockery of the entire family. *Felipe.*" His name was a command to bend to her will.

"Look on the bright side, Mother. He might win. You'll finally see your favorite on the throne." He nodded at his head of security to examine both swords before Francois's guard was given first choice of the weapons.

Queen Paloma stood taller, her hands curled

into fists, but she didn't contradict him. She didn't say she *didn't* want Francois to take the throne. She didn't tell Francois not to fight.

Still standing on opposite sides of the courtyard from his twin, Felipe accepted the sword that was brought to him. Its double-edged blade had been freshly sharpened and polished. He gripped the handle that was wrapped in soft leather, then drew a figure-eight with his wrist, testing the sword's weight and balance.

"What's this? You're not even dressed yet," King Enzo grumbled as he came out to the courtyard. "I was going to keep score myself. Best of five should do it."

"This is not a game, Padre. There will be no protective gear." Felipe moved toward the middle of the courtyard that would serve as their *piste*. "We fight until surrender. Or death, in my case, because I will not surrender."

"We'll see," Francois drawled as he approached. "You seem to have surrendered your wife without much struggle."

Felipe had no doubt that was how it looked to outsiders, but Felipe had Claudine within him. She filled him with strength. With power. With *will*. With a force greater than all of those things combined.

"Are you saying there are no rules at *all*?" the Queen cried.

"Even if there were, my dear brother would never play by them," Felipe said. No, he would have to be on guard against every type of underhanded cheating. "Prepare to lose one of your sons today, Mamma."

"You want everyone to believe you are better than me," Francois complained. "The fact is, you won't do what it takes to get the better of me. You're *weak*. That's why I deserve to be king and you do not."

"That's where you're wrong," Felipe assured him. "Exercising scruples isn't the same as being bound by them. But continue to underestimate me. That works to my advantage."

They each held out their swords and took up the *en garde* position, creeping forward until their swords began to engage.

For a few moments, they tested each other, barely moving beyond the flick of their blades in a very subtle parry and riposte, each trying to duck around the other's weapon. Each trying to make the other think he would attack from one side, only to quickly move to the other.

Felipe watched Francois as closely as he watched the movement of his sword, judging his reaction time, his level of arrogance. Felipe's contempt for Francois did not mean he failed to see him as dangerous. Quite the opposite. Despite a profligate lifestyle, Francois's reflexes were sharp.

He wanted this. He relished the chance to finally take Felipe down. Felipe had no doubt his brother would run him through, given a split second of lost focus.

What Francois didn't believe was that Felipe would do the same, if he had to.

Felipe tapped a little harder on Francois's blade. His twin reacted in a feint that Felipe countered, but he was equally ready for Francois to turn it into a genuine attack from another angle—which he did.

Felipe swung his blade in a swift arc to parry Francois. The clash of steel rang across the courtyard, making the Queen's gasp nearly inaudible.

They were closer now, moving like waltzing partners, holding the distance between them, each with one arm protectively tucked behind his back while they shifted their weight backward and forward in their lunge.

The clip and scrape of their *schiavonas'* steel became a steady, uneven clatter.

This was a warm-up as they both moved with increasing speed, each attempting to surprise the other with a thrust and throwing up a defense, then swooping into a fresh attack.

"You realize, don't you…" Francois was trying to sound lazy and unbothered, but they were both beginning to sweat from the exertion. "That *you* called *me* out. If I kill you, it's self-defense."

"You still won't have the throne, though. Claudine is pregnant." His declaration did what Felipe had hoped it would.

Francois faltered just enough for Felipe to catch him off guard. He thrust, slicing through Francois's trousers and into his thigh.

It would have gone deeper, but Francois swung his blade down to deflect the worst of it and quickly parried Felipe's follow-up thrust.

For a few moments, they clacked and clattered their swords, using more force now. They advanced and retreated, circling, each rattling his blade against the other's once again as they searched for an opening, keeping their movements small to conserve energy.

"After you're dead, I'll marry her and raise your—"

Felipe had been waiting for that threat. He feinted a lunge as though reacting with emotion. He allowed Francois to block it, then used the force of the parry to swing up his blade and swipe the tip of his blade across Francois's chin.

Francois jerked his head back, then lunged in the next second, aiming for Felipe's shoulder. He grazed Felipe's upper arm, but Felipe pivoted a quarter turn, sidestepping the worst of it, then used this new angle to take advantage of Francois's position. His sliced a line across Francois's waist even as his brother took another jab at him.

There was a shout of anguish from the Queen.

Blood was dripping from his brother's thigh and chin. Felipe was distantly aware of various burns and stings on his own body, particularly his upper arm. He didn't pause or show any mercy, however. He was utterly focused on the fear edging into his brother's eyes.

Francois began to hack with more panic than skill. The noise of their blades clanged unrelentingly in Felipe's ear as he grimly fought Francois off. He took no comfort in his brother's desperation. It made Francois all the more unpredictable and dangerous.

There were no rules. This was a fight to the death.

They were close enough, and the blades sharp enough, that they were both picking up nicks and cuts. And they were both moving fast enough, with enough force, that they were equally winded.

"Surrender," Felipe commanded.

"Nev—" Francois roared a curse as Felipe scored another line against his brother's arm.

Felipe had him on the defensive. He kept advancing, pushing him backward.

Francois's arm had to be aching as much as his own. Felipe's grip was slippery with sweat and he was breathing as though he'd been running for miles, but he drew on the well of endurance that had brought Claudine to his island. *Her* life and the life of their baby depended on this.

He continued to push Francois with inexorable purpose, until his brother turned his ankle and fell onto his back.

Francois thrust his sword up to defend himself, slashing pain across Felipe's hip, but Felipe parried and lunged forward, standing on his brother's arm until the sword clattered to the cobblestones.

He held Francois on his back with the point of his blade against Francois's throat.

"Felipe!" his mother screamed.

"Renounce your claim to the throne," Felipe demanded.

Francois slid his gaze past Felipe.

In his periphery, Felipe saw his mother's blue-gray skirt and his father's pin-striped trousers.

"Enzo, *please*," their mother begged.

"You are not fit to wear the crown." Felipe didn't step off his brother. He gave him another pinprick under his jaw. "Admit it. Renounce your claim. Say it loudly enough for everyone in this courtyard to hear it. Swear it to our king and queen."

"Padre," Francois beseeched, begging for mercy.

"I have no reason to spare his life," Felipe said heavily to their father. "He will only keep challenging me for the throne, we all know that. It ends here. You decide how."

"Don't kill him." Enzo touched his arm and sighed heavily. "I will abdicate the throne to you."

"As King, I will see that he faces the charges leveled against him," Felipe said clearly.

"As King, you may do as you see fit." Their father sounded infinitely weary, but relieved. "You may acknowledge Francois after this," he said to the Queen, "but I never will. Francois is no longer welcome in the palace," he called out to the palace guards. "He is no longer my son. Remove him and never grant him entry again."

It was a pronouncement as brutally harsh as their father had always been. Felipe's only pity was for the children who had once looked to that man as a guiding light only to find he was ruled by power and duty and not one iota of heart.

"Take his sword," Felipe said to Vinicio, not trusting Francois for even one second.

Vinicio quickly picked it up from the cobblestones.

Felipe remained armed even while Francois was escorted to his car.

The Queen followed her favorite son, crying, "I'll talk to him. Don't worry."

Felipe watched his mother ignore that he was equally exhausted and covered in cuts that bled freely, staining his clothes. She didn't once look back at him.

He sheathed his sword, keeping it as he went to his helicopter.

He flew back to Sentinella alone.

"You should have watched with me," Ann-Marie said.

"Watched what?" Claudine looked up from sweeping flower petals off the path down to the helicopter pad where they had landed shortly after Freja's husband, Giovanni, had arranged to take her to a secure location.

This remote villa in the Italian Alps was secure all right. Claudine supposed someone could hike in, if they knew it was here, but it would take days. All the supplies were flown in and it ran on solar, but it was not the least bit rustic. It was incredibly luxurious and built to accommodate a wheelchair, suggesting it was Giovanni's secret lair. It even had caretakers who kept urging her to relax and enjoy the nearby walking trails, but Claudine preferred to keep busy.

"The coronation ceremony," her mother said with a lilt of exasperation.

"Oh. That."

"That? Your husband is a king, Claudine. Enzo was there. He looks quite ill."

"He is," she murmured and went back to what she was doing.

"Honestly, Claudine, this can't go on. You're pining yourself into a decline."

She wasn't pining, exactly. She was doing the equivalent of walking the meditative maze, sweeping a long, winding path that she knew would be littered with petals in an hour, accepting that her actions were irrelevant and her fate inevitable.

She would have to go back to Felipe, even though he hadn't tried to stop her leaving him. Even though he hadn't reached out to so much as ask if she was still alive. When she had tried to talk to Giovanni about money, he had said that Felipe had already told him he would cover all costs.

Was her husband *glad* to have her out of sight and out of mind?

"I spoke to Giovanni," her mother continued. "He said that Francois has been cut off and cast out. The buyer for the pageant backed out. Francois has sold his yacht to pay legal fees, so he's stuck in Montenegro. If he goes anywhere else, he'll be extradited. The charges against him have grown, by the way. Five more women have come forward."

"Good." She supposed. Claudine didn't know how to feel about it. Validated? She'd rather no one else had suffered at Francois's hands, but at least her coming forward had provided an avenue that seemed safe enough for other women to tell their stories and hopefully find some sort of justice or closure.

"Giovanni said it would be safe for us to return to New York if that's what you want. We don't have to keep hiding here," her mother prodded.

Claudine sighed. She *was* hiding, mostly from herself. From the weakness in her that yearned for Felipe no matter how fraught her life was when she lived inside his world. She could bear the restrictions and the weight of his responsibilities and even his mother's dislike.

What she couldn't bear was the isolation within their marriage, the one that left her feeling alone in it.

She couldn't avoid him forever, though. Not when she was carrying the next heir to Nazarine. Tears of joy pressed behind her eyes every time she thought of her baby, but what kind of life would their child have if their father didn't love them? She had seen what that had done to Felipe.

Turning the ruby ring on her finger, she asked herself, *What would Queen Giulia do?*

She wouldn't run away, Claudine realized. No, despite all her trials, Queen Giulia had found a way to live a very difficult life on her own terms.

With a nod, Claudine started back to the house.

Felipe had achieved what was necessary for the health of his country, but there was no satisfaction in it. His mother was barely speaking to him and his father was not likely to last the year.

Enzo had mentioned more than once that Felipe should reconcile with Claudine and Felipe couldn't argue with him, but he couldn't ask Claudine to come back to him, either. Given what he'd put her through, it had to be her decision.

He missed her, though. He missed her and he wanted to know that their baby was well.

He moved through the duties of his station because it helped him push through the hours of the day, but he was so hollow and empty of purpose he wondered what the point was in living at all. He felt as though he lacked something vital to his survival. He had air and water and food and sunlight, but he didn't care about any of it.

A murmur went through the crowd around him, forcing him to recall he was in Rome at a charity gala. Why? He couldn't recall what organization it benefited or why he'd agreed to speak or even what he was supposed to say. He would rather not be here at all.

He glanced around and realized people were staring at him and then turning their heads to look at—

He caught his breath. Life flowed back into him the way water soaked into a desiccated sponge. The music no longer blended into the din of conversation. It suddenly sounded beautiful and alluring. The stale air developed notes of seafood and puff pastry, perfumes and aftershaves. The icy crystals in the chandelier refracted to project streaks of bright yellow and deep blue.

Every step she took toward him filled him with oxygen and ferocity and gladness. With something glowing and meaningful. Something necessary to his very existence.

Claudine was a vision in a dark blue gown that fell down her figure like a coat of paint. A swirl of white hung off one shoulder, adding laconic elegance to the look. Her hair was up, exposing her long, bare neck.

There was no hesitation in her steps as she approached him. She looked straight at him, reminding him of how she'd come down the aisle toward him, so confident on their wedding day and so weak the last time he'd seen her.

When she was close enough to speak, she said only, "Felipe."

"Claudine." Her name was a vibration inside his breastbone. A call. Every cell in his body was trying to sync with hers. God, he had missed her. "What are you doing here?"

"Showing my support for the preservation of the Mediterranean ecosystem. You?"

Waiting for you.

That was what he wanted to say, even though it was whimsical and wistful and far more sentimental than he knew how to be.

"Your Majesty," Vinicio greeted her with a deferential nod. He was no doubt having a subtle conniption that he hadn't known Claudine would be here.

"Majesty?" She looked up at Felipe. "But your mother—"

"Has a new title. *You* are Queen of Nazarine. Shall we dance?" He ached to touch her.

She mutely let him take her hand and lead her onto the floor.

He could have crushed her, he wanted so badly to absorb her into his skin, but he made himself lock his arms in a civilized embrace.

"We need to talk about some things," she said.

"If you're here to ask for a divorce, I've instructed my lawyers to negotiate in good faith."

Her step faltered.

He steadied her and noted the way her face had paled. Was she well? The baby? His blood congealed with fear in his veins.

"There are things they're not in a position to give me," she said cryptically.

"Such as?"

Her brow furrowed with frustration. "I want your heart, Felipe."

"On a silver platter?" he said on a husk of a laugh, tempted to say, *You have it.*

Everything in him went very still. He stopped moving as realization poured through him. *That* was why he had been feeling so empty. She had taken his heart when she left. He loved her.

He stood there with his eyes closed, absorbing that stunning realization, utterly speechless as understanding of that emotion finally exploded through him. It was esteem and loyalty and admiration and so many more things than she had described. It was beauty and affection and faith and joyous laughter.

"Please don't make jokes." Her mouth quivered and she looked down at the ruffles on his shirt.

He could only blink in bemusement at her, utterly thrown by what was happening to him. But a remarkable tenderness was rising in him like a king tide.

"I shouldn't have done this here," she continued under her breath. "I thought I could be bold and brave. I thought I could be in control for a change."

"Do you really think I've ever been in control where you're concerned?" he scoffed.

Cupid's arrow had pierced him the moment he saw her. He remembered it clearly, yet it was such a foreign concept that he had dismissed it as lust and fascination. Those things didn't leave you feeling as though you were bleeding out when you were apart, though. Only love could have made him suffer this intensely.

"People are staring," she said, aggrieved. "I have a room upstairs. Can we talk there?"

"We'll go to mine." He cradled her elbow and the crowd parted as they made their way to the elevators.

He was pleased to see she had a bodyguard shadowing her—one who had previously worked for him. Vinicio and his own guard for the evening joined them as they waited for the elevator and the three men nodded a friendly greeting at each other.

The doors opened and the startled occupants slipped past them, allowing them to enter the empty car.

Felipe took her hand and drew her to the back, unable to stop staring at her. She was magnificent. She was *here*.

She looked up at him and a soft noise that was anguish and helplessness and relief left her as she pressed herself into him, sliding her arms around his waist as though she had every right. Which she did. He was hers in every way that mattered.

Her yearning gaze matched the longing that stretched out inside him. Her mouth lifted in invitation and her hand went to the back of his head, urging him to kiss her.

Catching her close with one arm, he cradled the back of her skull with his free hand, covered her mouth with his own. Then he stole back every kiss he had missed while she'd been gone. No matter how hard he tried, he would never be able to kiss her thoroughly enough, or hold her closely enough, or fill her deeply enough, to quell this need in him for her.

The elevator pinged and the doors opened. Vinicio stepped out and the two guards shifted to stand in the opening, forming a wall of privacy while freezing the elevator in place.

Felipe could have made love to her right here. He wanted to. Badly. But she was already drawing away, blinking and glancing self-consciously at the backs of their guards. She touched her mouth where her lipstick was smudged, looking contrite.

That had nearly got out of hand! Claudine was mortified.

Felipe offered his pocket square and cleared his throat. The guards shifted and Vinicio led them down the hall to the sort of presidential suite Felipe always occupied when he was in Rome. The guard who was stationed at the door brightened when he saw her and gave her a nod of greeting.

"Will you be need—" Vinicio began.

"No," Felipe interjected. "Good night."

He closed them into his suite so abruptly it bordered on rude.

He reached for Claudine, but she held up a hand and took a couple of steps backward. She was still running his white pocket square around her mouth. She found a mirror and glanced to see she had erased as much as she could.

"It's only the two of us here," Felipe assured her. "I couldn't care less how you look."

"I know, but…" She shook that off and came closer to offer the stained silk back to him. "How, um, how are your parents?"

"Sick." He discarded the square onto a side table. "One physically, the other emotionally. I can't do anything about either."

She took that to mean his mother was still favoring Francois and still blaming Felipe for the trouble his twin was in.

"Are you angry?" she asked.

"I can't remember a time when I wasn't," he said flatly. He moved to pour himself a brandy.

"At me, I mean."

"No." He paused in pouring. His profile grew reflective. "Yes," he amended. "I don't want to be, but I am."

"Because I left? You think I'm a coward?"

"No." His laugh was a rasp of dark humor as he picked up his glass. "No, I think you are the bravest, toughest, most exceptional person I know."

"Even though I ran away?"

"You didn't, though. You did what any mother would do. You took our unborn baby to safety. Didn't you?" He turned and pinned her with his stare, the force of it so piercing she caught a shaken breath.

Her hand went reflexively to her abdomen. "I had to. It wasn't about not trusting you. I didn't trust him. Or your parents. I couldn't take the risk that they would side with him again."

"I know. I know that you would have fought him alongside me if it was only yourself you were worried about. You weren't even protecting our future ruler, were you? You were simply protecting a helpless baby. *Our* baby." He seemed to need a drink to chase that acknowledgement. He gulped. "Is everything well? How are you feeling?"

"Fine." She clasped her elbows. She had seen a doctor here in Rome when she landed, to be sure everything was as it should be, and it was.

"You look apprehensive. Why? Francois has been neutralized. Any staff who ever showed a hint of fealty toward him has been culled from the payroll. The palace is completely safe. You don't even need to see my parents if you come back. My father is accepting hospice care on Sentinella. Mother is having the *vedova* villa on Stella Vista redecorated so it will be ready for her after he's gone."

"I'm so sorry, Felipe." She searched his hard features. "Are you upset at all? Beginning to grieve or…anything?"

"Grief comes from losing someone you love."

"And you told me a long time ago that you didn't believe in love." *That* was why she was apprehensive.

"I didn't," he agreed solemnly. "Until I grieved the fact that you were absent from my life."

Her heart swerved. A small soar of hope rose in her, but she fought it back.

"Please don't say anything you don't mean. I'm prepared to come back. I know I have to. Our baby deserves to know his or her father."

"Our baby is entitled to the throne," he pointed out.

"Our baby is entitled to be loved." Her insides shook as she said it, but she rooted her feet as she added, "As am I."

"What do you think I have just said to you, *cara mia*?" He took a step toward her.

"I think you are saying what you think needs to be said to bring your child into the palace." She held up a hand to stave him off. "I need your honesty more than ever, Felipe. I'm only asking that you promise me you will *try* to open your heart to us. I can't trust you if you lie to me now."

"Tell me first why you left. You didn't trust me to keep you both safe, did you? I failed you. I did. I will never forgive myself for that and I will never make that mistake again. But I don't think that's why you left. Is it?"

She shook her head. "I knew we were a liability for you. That as long as he could attack you through me, he would."

"I don't think that was it, either." He nodded thoughtfully as he ambled closer. "I think you were forcing me to make a choice."

"Not between the crown and me," she cried. "I know that's not fair."

"Between bitterness and love." He drained his glass and set it aside. "Between the life I was told I had to accept and the future I could have with you, if I was prepared to fight for it."

"I didn't expect you to duel him, Felipe." She searched across his frame, looking for injuries. "The reports said you both had several cuts."

"Cuts, yes. Nothing compared to the way you carved out my heart then left with it."

"That's not f—"

"No. Listen." He captured her hands. "Try to imagine never being loved, Claudine. Not for one moment in your whole life. There was a little affection when I was very young—a kind nanny. An aunt who gave me sweets and told me stories, but my mother preferred my brother and my brother hated my guts. My father never had a thought in his life that was not wrapped up in duty to the crown and I was told to emulate that. Now imagine you have found a sort of comfort in that vacuum of true caring. You understand how it works the way people learn to exist in the arctic. Then along comes someone who radiates love. Who pours it over you. I didn't even know what it *was*, Claudine. Sex? Charisma? A needy child finally tasting what it is to be noticed? Nothing made sense."

She tilted her head, so anguished for that child he'd been. For the man who'd had to learn to live in isolation and like it.

"I accept your pity. I accept your mistrust of the man who saw you as someone who was useful, rather than the person who would save him, not from his cold family, but from his own cynicism. I was determined to remain autonomous. It was comfortable. Loving you *hurts*, Claudine. Every part of me is unprotected because you are walking in this cruel world, susceptible to harm. Whether it's my vindictive brother or a mosquito, I don't want anything to touch you because that will hurt *me*. It terrifies me to be this vulnerable."

He was crushing her hands, but she didn't protest. She only clung right back, letting him know he wasn't alone anymore. He never would be again.

"But I can't go back to that life of emptiness. You can have my heart because I have yours. I know I have it because I feel it inside me. It's soft and endlessly warm and fills me with light. I am keeping it, Claudine. It's *mine*."

She had to bite her lips because they were quivering so hard.

"Will you take mine in return?" he asked humbly. "Please? It's small and hard and will need a lot of tending to make it grow, but I know you can make it happen. I know I will be a better man for it."

"Oh, Felipe." She was blinking her wet eyes as she thrust herself into his arms. "I love you so much."

"God knows why you do, but I will take all that you'll give me." He scooped her up and carried her into the bedroom.

"Not the sofa?" she teased as she looped her arms around his neck. "Even the floor has served us well in the past."

"You're pregnant." He frowned in a small scold, then his mouth kicked to the side. "Also, I'd have to carry you to bed after so it's better to get it out of the way while I still have my strength." He came down onto the wide mattress with her and carried her ring hand to his lips. "I do love you, Claudine." His face flexed with emotion. "I don't know why I feared saying it. It fills me with power to tell you. With a certainty that I can and will do anything for *us*." His hand slid to her abdomen. "All of us."

They kissed as though sealing the promise. Hot

tears spilled from her eyes, it was such a fiercely sweet benediction.

Passion mingled with this new, profound tenderness, slowing them down. As they kissed and undressed each other, their caresses were unhurried and sure, imbued with caring. With need and admiration and love.

When they were naked and he shifted to settle between her legs, she cradled him with her thighs and welcomed his intrusion with a blissful sigh of utter contentment. With supreme rightness.

They stayed like that a long time, barely moving, enjoying the sensation of being joined while still pouring affection on each other. A trailing touch here, a chain of kisses there.

"I've never felt so free as when I'm with you like this," she murmured.

"I've never felt so alive. You *are* my life, Claudine. Never believe otherwise," Felipe told her.

He began to move with more purpose. When climax arrived, it was a startlingly new pinnacle, one intensified by the naked emotion between them, melding them together as they tumbled through the cosmos. Joined. Forever.

EPILOGUE

Four years later

"How are you, my love?" Felipe's voice still had the power to make her skin tighten and her pulse ripple when he caught her unawares like this.

She covered the hand that came to rest on her shoulder and tilted her head back for his kiss, but didn't rise from her comfortable position on the lounger.

"You're finished early."

"We have places to be, don't we?" He leaned down to kiss her and gave her swollen belly a caress of greeting. "Unless you have your own work to finish?"

"Not right this minute." She set aside the tablet she'd been holding.

For the last three years, she'd been working on finding, transcribing, editing and translating Queen Giulia's many notes, essays, letters and other writings. The first volume was finally at a copy edit stage and would be published next year—if she managed to finish her corrections before this baby was born. She still had two months to go, though.

"Papà!" Romeo cried, noticing him. "Rico!" he called to his brother as he started to run. "Papà is here." He paused to wait while Rico leaped up from the sandbox to hurry after him.

They were three and a half and near impossible for anyone but their parents to tell apart. Aside from her and Felipe, only the late Dr. Esposito knew which boy had been born first.

Rico fell and his small cry of surprise had Romeo stopping in his tracks. He ran back.

"Are you hurt?" He dropped to kneel beside his brother.

Rico sat up and clutched his knee, blowing on it.

"I've got it." Felipe squeezed her shoulder, urging her to stay on the lounger as he strode toward the boys.

It never ceased to swell her heart when she saw him dote on their children this way.

"Let me see." He crouched and gathered Rico up to examine the tear in his pants. "No blood. I think you'll survive." He kissed the boy's hair.

"You have to kiss his knee, Papà," Romeo explained. "To make it better."

"Of course." He playfully swung Rico upside

down to do it, dispelling the last of Rico's upset into a gale of laughter.

Now Romeo wanted to be part of the silliness and fell on them. Felipe tipped onto the grass as though bowled over by the small boy. He wrestled with them like an alpha wolf with a pair of cubs.

When he had worn them out sufficiently, he sat up, both boys secured in his strong arms. "Are we going to Sentinella or not?"

"Sì!" they cried and tried to get away, but he kept hold of them, causing more giggling and cries for "Mamma. Help!"

"Are you not coming?" she called as she rose. "I don't want to go all by myself."

"No. Mamma, wait! Papà, let *go.*"

They all loved their time at Sentinella where they were alone, but together.

Felipe released them and they ran toward the helipad, glancing back to ensure their parents were following.

Felipe waited for her, hand outstretched. When she came alongside him, he slid his hand beneath her hair to cradle the back of her neck, gaze still on their boys as they paused at the fence, as they had been taught to do. They once again examined the tear in Rico's pants, but now it was something that made them giggle.

"I do love you, you know," he said, gaze troubled, as though he was searching for stronger words to impress that truth into her. "I could not have taught them to love each other that much if you had not taught me to feel it. I love you more than I know how to express."

"It's okay. I believe you," she assured him, snuggling herself into his side. "I love you, too."

* * * * *

Were you head over heels for
Awakened on Her Royal Wedding Night?
Then don't miss these other stories
by Dani Collins!

Innocent in Her Enemy's Bed
Cinderella's Secret Baby
Wedding Night with the Wrong Billionaire
A Convenient Ring to Claim Her
A Baby to Make Her His Bride

Available now!